METROPOLICKS Book 2:
Adventures in Dating

Felicia Lin and Victor Scott Rodriguez

WWS Press
New York

WWS Press
Metropolicks Book 2: Adventures in Dating
Felicia Lin and Victor Scott Rodriguez

Published in the United States of America by WWS Press
ISBN 978-0-9907768-4-0

Printed by Create Space, a DBA of On-Demand Publishing LLC

Metropolicks*
[mi-trop-uh-liks]

noun

1. A large, busy international city (e.g. New York City) filled with varied stories of relationship adventures and misadventures.

2. A major urban center in which sexual activity is prominent, especially those involving the use of one's tongue.

3. A fast-paced, competitive metropolis where highly ambitious people focus on licking the competition and getting ahead in dating.

* as defined on The Urban Dictionary

FOR MORE ON METROPOLICKS VISIT:
www.Metropolicks.com

ACKNOWLEDGMENTS

Writing a book is one thing, but creating a finished product is another. There are indeed many people to thank and acknowledge for making this book series happen. It is hard to know where to begin.

Thank you to Alice Heiserman, our diligent, enthusiastic content and copy editor, who added much value to the novel. We owe you a great deal.

We'd also like to acknowledge the contributions of those who gave us insights, each in their own way, into the mechanics and legalities of self-publishing: Hugh Howey, Guy Kawasaki and Shawn Welch, Maria Murnane, and Rob Thony.

Many thanks to the several romance authors who shared their experience and advice with us including: Tina DeSalvo, Debra Holland, Beverly Jenkins, Diane Kelly, Maggie Marr, Tessa McFionn, Sarah MacLean, Priscilla Oliveras, Maggie Rivers, and Cecilia Tan.

Much appreciation goes to those who offered advice and recommendations regarding the cover designs of the book series, among them are: Candace Braun Davison, Serena Chen, Joanne Louie, Johanna Salazar, and Peter Yang Zhao.

We are grateful to Vinny Bove, Emily Chen, George Madarasz, and Michelle Shinagawa for your recommendations and expertise in making our book covers come to life. A big thank you also goes to Gilly Rosenthol, who formatted our book series. We'd also like to thank Jennie Yip and Claudine Lee who created a one-of-a-kind artwork that appears in the Metropolicks ebook.

A big debt of thanks goes to Maggie Law, our talented photographer, who tirelessly photographed several models during a marathon shoot. Among the models are: Jide Alao, Sarah Clark, Ryan Dawalt, Mieko Gavia, Jason He, Lynda Hinder, Kara Xinhang Li, Andrew Nicholas, Prakash Patil, David Rodriguez, Gabby Jiayin She, Tina Telalyan, and Pai-Sen Wang. Each one of you brought something truly unique to the shoot and your photos have been used for our promotional campaigns. But we do want to especially thank Davide Filippini and Sheila G., our Metropolicks Books 1-3 cover models. The chemistry between the two of you, as seen in your photos and the Metropolicks videos, is undeniable. Other people to thank regarding the photo shoot include: Kristin Mirabelle, our hair and makeup artist, Alice Chin, our wardrobe consultant, and the rest of the crew: Huaying Chen, Deanna Denman, Annie Lu, Sara Vinik, and Tony Wong.

We are grateful to Jami Jackson, Caesar Jackson and Blacque Records for sharing Jami's musical talent with us. Jami's songs "Let Love Live" and "Keep Walkin' On" have been featured in two Metropolicks music videos with the behind the scenes footage from the photo shoot.

And before all of this, there were our test readers. Thank you; you were the first ones to give us feedback and perspective on the novel.

We also want to specifically acknowledge the following people for their support and friendship: Juan Betancourt, David Chan, Will Chao, Nicole Chen, Donna Drake, Diana Lee, Jack Li, Supei Liu, Joanne Louie, Diana Mao, Alissa Moore, Chris Nicodemo, Krista Sande-Kerback, Nelson Searcy, Ryan Shemen, Jim Su, Kerrick Thomas, Lorie Thomas, Yue Wang, and Cindy Zhou.

And lastly, thank you to Catarina Serra and Ichi Shih for hosting a Halloween party several years ago, where we met each other for the very first time. The rest, as they say, is history.

Felicia and Victor

TABLE OF CONTENTS

YEAR II: SUMMER

YEAR II: FALL

INTRODUCTION

Dating in New York is not for the faint of heart. With so many singles packed into the island of Manhattan and people marrying later in life, you'd think that there would be endless opportunities to find love. However, with so many options, it is easy to find yourself going through the revolving doors of dating. There are always fresh distractions—the newer, the better, or the trendier. Who has the time or patience to make relationships work? So, are the odds really in your favor in New York if you are looking for Mr. or Ms. Right?

To have a fighting chance you'll need a plan of attack and a support system. In fact, you'll need all the help you can get. You'll need an army to win this war. This army includes your friends, those you can trust, those who you can go to with the joy and the pain of your pursuit. Don't forget your friends' friends, and your acquaintances—you never know who you'll meet through these connections. And then, you will need a backup plan. So, suit up, put on your best armor—be it a little black dress or your sharpest looking suit. Lock and load your best pickup lines or your sexiest, most charming smile, because love is a battlefield. And as the saying goes, you may have to kiss a lot of frogs before you find your prince or princess.

When you are single and have lived in New York long enough, you will probably have a few stories to share. We soon found out that this was truer than we could have imagined. As friends heard that we were working on this novel, a strange thing began happening. People started volunteering to share their dating stories with us.

While our novel was inspired in part by people's true dating experiences in New York City, these experiences were used in a fictitious manner. The novel is a work of fiction and is a result of our creative imagination. Our intention was to create characters who were composites. Therefore, any resemblance to real persons, living or dead, is purely coincidental and unintentional.

Another unusual development happened during the writing of this book—when someone gave us legal consent to be mentioned in the book by name, with the caveat that none of that individual's personal stories be included in the book. That led to several other people being mentioned in the book by their real names, and we followed the same protocol with each of them. Thus, the stories in this book are interspersed with the names of real people and real places.

There are many stories to be told and others that are best kept private. We are here to tell the tales of a few New Yorkers brave enough to endure heartbreak and rejection in order to find love. In the words of the great poet Ovid, "Fortune and love favor the brave."

We wish to thank all who have contributed stories, but, of course, we can't do so by name. In order to protect people's anonymity, we have changed names, ethnicities, occupations, places of residence and identifiable physical characteristics, and in some instances, the gender, national origin, religious views, and political views of those who have volunteered stories. In every instance, we have combined several stories within the same chapter, so that every chapter is in fact composite in nature.

One last thought: when a dating relationship goes awry, don't sweat it; it is not the end of the world. How do we know it is not the end of the world? Because it is already tomorrow in Taiwan.

YEAR II

SPRING

Me Horny, You Available?

(LUANA)

I always liked the *Tarzan* movies. He was just so primitive, but he actually had a good heart. "Me Tarzan, you Jane" is a classic movie line. It's simple, yet effective. Try something like that the next time you go to a bar, like "Me horny, you available?" and I'll bet the man you say that to leaves the bar with you that instant.

My friend Mark reminded me of Tarzan. He was one of those men who could rock the stubble. It made him look even sexier than when he was clean-shaven. Formerly an exotic dancer, he had hundreds of women each night stroking his dick and stuffing dollars into his thong. He was hung like a horse and was the only guy I know who was always hard. He said that he took a combination of horny goat weed, avena sativa, and cordyceps and the result was that he was as hard as a glass dildo.

I would get together with him whenever I was in the mood for some sexual adventure. I knew that I could always count on him for a good lay. Mark was always up for something. He wasn't interested in any permanent relationship. He just liked to have sex. Plain and simple, like Tarzan.

I love the burlesque revival that's happening in New York. From semi-nude to completely nude, the shows are elegant and titillating. But it really isn't a place to get hit on by guys. Most guys come with dates, and some of the single guys are on the creepy side. So, I would always go with Mark. Our favorite performer was a curvaceous brunette who would spank herself with a paddle, with an enthusiasm usually only seen displayed by Amway sales reps or Scientologists.

Mark was also the one who went with me to a nudist colony. We were really disappointed to find out that it was actually more of a family thing! There were lots of middle-aged and out-of-shape men and women and even families with babies, if you can believe it.

I guess Mark and I were too hot for the nudists. Every woman who saw Mark would stare at him longingly. Mark wasn't fazed by it at all, of course. I guess size does matter in certain situations. On the flip side, every guy who saw me got a hard on, which didn't always go over too well with his wife. Why? Well, I go to the gym seven days a week and go to spas for my skin to look supple. I always get a nice bikini wax so I have my little airstrip for the guys to land on. My tits are perfect (if I do say so myself), definitely above average in size, all natural and my nipples are perfect for any mamma's boy out there who wasn't breastfed enough as a kid. So, while I had expected to see something like an orgy from Caligula's court, instead, I ended up getting the nude *Family Guy*.

Yes, you name it, I've tried it or I will. One of the most memorable was this swingers club that Mark told me about. Women were allowed to come in by themselves but a man had to be with a woman in order to get in. I was curious, so we went together. When Mark and I arrived at the club, we walked down some steps and then we were directed to a unisex locker room where we took off all of our clothes and put on a towel sans underwear.

Next, we entered this giant orgy room with people everywhere having sex and moaning and groaning. We joined a group of onlookers who were staring at another group of couples on the floor of this giant room. Men going down on women, threesomes, women giving blow jobs and hand jobs, couples in the missionary position, women-on-top position, doggy style, you name it. We went into another section where there was a private room. I was really horny by then, and Mark, well he's always ready. So of course, Mark and I had sex. I still wonder what it would have been like if we had actually done it in the orgy room. I'm sure that if that had happened, it wouldn't have involved just the two of us then.

We also gave the BDSM party circuit a shot. I dressed as a dominatrix and Mark was the submissive. I put a leash on his neck. It's all about obedience at BDSM parties and they have their own version of fetish etiquette or what I like to call "fetiquette." Rule number one, you should always ask first if you would like to touch or spank someone. So, you'll hear lots of "yes sirs" and "yes mistresses." But it also wasn't really my type of place since after the first time you spank a guy, it gets a little boring. Maybe mixing up the power dynamic and making it unpredictable would make things more interesting.

And then three months passed. I hadn't seen Mark and the next time I called him up, I was surprised when he told me that he had gotten engaged to a petite public school teacher. She, of course, couldn't get enough of Mark and rarely let him out of her sight.

Though Mark had told me he was now engaged, he suggested that we get together again soon, expecting us to continue just as before. I guess he thought Tarzan's companion was named "cheater" instead of cheetah. But after all the pain my ex-boyfriend Gianni caused me, I couldn't do that to Mark's fiancé. Even though Mark was for sex and only for sex, I had his fiancé's feelings to consider, so I decided against seeing him again.

Double Booking

(KATIA)

Katia was looking for an upgrade. Katia was still with Donovan, the investment banker, but their relationship had gotten stale. Lately, she had been feeling like she was not getting enough time with Donovan, which seemed ridiculous because she was effectively living with him, even though she had her own gorgeous 3,500 square foot apartment on the Upper East Side. Katia had gotten the apartment as part of the settlement in her divorce a few years ago.

Katia's Story:

In my mind, I have always kept my options open. Anyone who knows me knows that I am always on the lookout for a dumber and richer man who'd be able to maintain my lifestyle. I didn't want to waste any more time with Donovan, so I had started booking back-to-back dates with several different men.

Today, I was going to have a drink with Brad before meeting Donovan for dinner. Brad, an attorney, who I had met through Montoya, was the rugged outdoorsy type. He had recently moved from the West Coast to become chief legal counsel for a hedge fund. When we had met, he seemed very taken by me and immediately asked to see me again.

I was looking forward to getting to know Brad a bit more. The night we met, we had a great conversation about art and interiors. He was a beginner art collector and having just moved to New

York, he was thinking about how to do the interiors of a Tribeca loft apartment, which he had just purchased. As we talked, Brad realized that I had expertise in art. That's when I told him that I was an art dealer. At the end of the night, Brad said that he'd like to meet again to continue our conversation, but I thought that was just an excuse for him to see me again.

Today I was dressed in a white body-hugging dress, which revealed my curves and one of my bare shoulders. As I walked over to Brad, he stood up to greet me.

"Hello babe. You look gorgeous," he said as he kissed me on the cheek.

"Hello darling. So nice to see you again, too," I said.

Brad pulled out a chair for me at the bar, "What would you like to drink? Oh, I know, a glass of Dom Pérignon for the lady. I'll have a scotch on the rocks."

I looked at Brad and thought, it's too bad I'm going to have to keep this short since I have plans to meet Donovan for dinner later. I hadn't seen Donovan in weeks. But this could be interesting. It was like a little fishing expedition to learn more about Brad.

It turns out, Brad had modeled, been a semiprofessional triathlete, traveled the world, and now he was looking for a different sort of a challenge professionally.

He had a very competitive nature. Brad asked what my life had been like in Russia, which led me to tell him about my childhood in Russia. My family had lived hand to mouth, and I had vowed that I would find a way to get out and make a better life for myself.

As the conversation progressed, I realized that I needed to pace myself, so I said to Brad, "Darling, I have to be somewhere at eight, so, I'm sorry that I'm going to have to watch the time and might have to cut this a bit short."

"Sure, no problem," Brad said. "So, about my loft in Tribeca, I have the whole floor to myself, but I'm planning on doing some renovations on it first, especially with the bathroom. I want to upgrade all of the fixtures and to put in a nice big bathtub that's big enough for two and for a nice relaxing soak at the end of a long day. I'm also going to have some rewiring done since it's a prewar building. With your expertise, I'd love to have you take a look at it and do the interiors. We can talk about your fees later. I want to make it feel like a home fit for a king."

I did not like this sudden shift in gears. I thought that this was supposed to be a date, not a business meeting.

Brad continued, "There are some restrictions on what I can do with it, of course, being a pre-war building and all, but I'd definitely want to preserve the apartment's character, so you should help me to furnish it and make it feel like home."

"Look, darling, that's not what I do. I'm an art dealer, not an interior decorator and no offense, but you wouldn't be able to afford me anyhow. I only work with very exclusive clients who make it worth my while."

I looked at my watch to check the time. It was about 7:30 P.M. "Oh, look at the time! It's been such a pleasure chatting with you, and as you know, I must get going now."

Brad's Story:

Besides having a curvy hourglass figure, Katia is a woman who knows about art. I knew this soon after we started a conversation. It's been a while since I've had a conversation like that about art. I am an avid art collector, but I was impressed by her knowledge. She talked about some of the art pieces that she had used to decorate her own apartment and how she had helped a friend of hers to renovate and decorate his apartment. Clearly, she has impeccable taste. I had just bought a loft in Tribeca and realized that I could really use her expertise. And, if I could give business to a friend of a friend, all the better.

So, I immediately asked her for her contact information so that we could meet again. I figured that we could have a friendly drink after work and I could tell her more about what I had in mind for my apartment. When we met for a drink, I got to know her a bit better and learned what makes her tick. I suppose the struggles she had as a child growing up in Russia are what's motivated her to make a better life for herself here in the U.S.

Then, when Katia said she had to be somewhere at eight, I realized I should get down to business, and that I'd still be able to meet up with Corrine later on. I was surprised at how Katia reacted when I asked her to do the interior decorating for my apartment. Her demeanor completely changed. She was obviously offended by the idea. I know that she's more of an art dealer, but I didn't think that she'd react this way. By contrast, Corrine is so much more easygoing.

Katia's Story:

I hopped into a taxi up to the Upper East Side, to meet Donovan for dinner, but he had not yet arrived. He was in some board meeting after which he said he'd head straight over to the restaurant to meet with me. It was not the first time he'd been late meeting me. With anyone else I normally wouldn't put up with this. It had not been like this in the beginning of the relationship. He had doted on me and had always been punctual, but now things had changed. I've been with this man for a year already, I thought.

One thing was for sure, I did feel secure; Donovan's money gave me a sense of security. Money was my security. It was the one thing that I always felt I could count on. As for love, well, I'm not so sure about that. People change, life changes; love isn't always enough, and it doesn't always last. If things don't work out, having money is a good consolation prize. At least money makes dealing with many of life's problems a little easier. I'd learned this from my divorce.

Donovan does take care of everything for me. When he's not around, I am free to do whatever I want, no questions asked. But I like companionship, not just the feeling of having someone else take care of me. I certainly have enough money to be comfortable on my own, but if I ever got married again, I'd have to give up my alimony. So, I'm looking for a man with money who is happy to take care of me, able to maintain my lifestyle, and be my companion. But lately, I've been wondering if Donovan is that man.

The maître d' greeted me and immediately escorted me to a table Donovan had reserved. I knew that Donovan would show up eventually, but, until then, I would have to wait. The wait staff brought me a glass of Dom Pérignon, courtesy of Donovan. From the table, I could discretely observe what was going on around the restaurant and at the bar, since I was hidden from the view of others.

As I sipped my drink, I saw Brad walk in through the entrance by the bar section. Of all the places he could've gone to grab a drink, he had to end up here. What were the odds of this happening? Before I even had a chance to wonder what he was doing here, a tall, striking, blonde woman, tall enough and thin enough to be a runway model, walked in through the same door. Brad saw the blonde, immediately stood up, and walked over to her. The two embraced warmly. As they did so, the woman seemed to be whispering something in Brad's ear. They looked at each other, laughed, and then leaned in to kiss. Brad took the woman's hand, led her to bar, and pulled out a chair for her. As they sat at the bar, they gazed deeply at each other as they talked.

Now, it was clear. My meeting with Brad had really been strictly for business. Apparently, he had also had a date lined up for later that evening. And from the looks of it, it was not something casual. I had completely misjudged Brad's intentions. As I sat waiting for Donovan, I started feeling more and more annoyed. It was as if I were being played for a fool for the second time that night.

Downing the rest of the Dom Pérignon, I decided that enough was enough. I got up and walked out of the restaurant. So what if Donovan arrived and found me not there? Who knows what time it would be when he finally arrived. He has kept me waiting plenty of times and even canceled on me before. But I don't need to stand for that. Let's see how he feels if the tables are turned. In the past he'd apologize by lavishing some expensive items on me, but I was tired of it. In the cab on the way back to Donovan's apartment, I decided to send Brad a text message with the name and number of an interior decorator with whom he could work.

Back at the apartment I started gathering all of my things. I emptied my walk-in closet, took all of my jewelry, and called a car service to transport me and my precious belongings back to my own apartment. Before leaving the apartment, I wrote a note for Donovan and left it on his nightstand. The note said:

Donovan,
I do like money, and a life of luxury, but what I really need is more than just that.
—Katia

Then I locked the door behind me and gave my key to the door-man. I asked him to give it to Donovan when he saw him next.

Brad's Story:

Corrine and I had agreed to meet later on the Upper East Side. So, it worked out that Katia had to be somewhere at eight. Corrine is quite a stunner. I had met her after she did a runway show for my friend, an up and coming fashion designer. Corrine and I have such amazing chemistry and we, of course, ended up back at her place at the end of the night.

I'm glad that in the end Katia came around and was kind enough to send me a referral for an interior designer who I might be able to work with.

Donovan's Story:

When I arrived at the restaurant, I was surprised when the maître d' told me that Katia had already been there and left. The nerve of her! I work my ass off for her and this is how much she appreciates it? After paying for the bottle of Dom Pérignon that she had ordered, I hailed a cab to go home. Once home, the doorman told me that Katia had left her key for me, and when I went into the bedroom, I saw that there was a note on the nightstand. I read the note and couldn't believe what I was reading. That bitch! How could she do this to me after how well I have treated her?! After I've showered her with expensive jewelry and gifts! In this city I'm sure it won't take me long to find someone else who appreciates what I have to offer.

The Cuddle Puddle

(LUANA)

A month after Mark had told me that he had gotten engaged, he called to tell me that he had broken up with his fiancée. At first I didn't believe him, but Mark said to check his list of friends on his *Facebook* page and that I'd see that his fiancée was no longer there. When I finally broke up with Gianni he deleted me from his *Facebook* friends list. Why do people you break up with want to delete you on *Facebook*? I guess it is because they don't want to see photos of you with somebody new. My thought is, if you've moved on already, then why should you care if I've found someone new? But then again, maybe they haven't moved on.

My friend, Jim Su, who is a body painter, invited me to a Burning Man party. So, I invited Mark along, now that he was unattached. Of all the places I've been with Mark, we did have a winner with the Burning Man parties.

When I invited Mark, he asked, "Is this party like the BDSM circuit where people must obey or get punished?"

"It isn't about obedience and punishment. At Burning Man, we are all just naughty," I told Mark mischievously. "But seriously, it isn't like a big orgy. It's just people having some fun."

As soon as we got to the party, we hit the dance floor. Our clothes glowed in the dark as we danced. I was wearing a green neon halter top and white bell bottom pants. Mark was wearing a white T-shirt and denim cut off shorts. The DJ that night was really on, and I found myself feeling mesmerized. There's a reason they call it trance music. I looked around at all of these beautiful bodies and beautiful people on the dance floor. Some of the men had started going shirtless. Just as I was thinking about taking off my top and joining them, I saw Jim painting a man's bicep with glow-in-the dark body paint. I grabbed Mark and said, "Let's go get painted by Jim."

That's what Jim did; he'd body paint men and women at all sorts of parties like masquerade and burlesque themed ones. Jim would paint the bare torsos of men and women. The human body was his canvas. I had Jim paint my tits and the paint made my nipples so hard I felt like I could put someone's eye out. Mark also went shirtless and Jim painted him too. As we continued dancing, our bodies glowed in the dark. The body paint was the only thing camouflaging our bare skin. Everything felt so primal.

Jim would take photos of some of his live artwork and put them up on *Facebook*. But he soon got a warning message from *Facebook* telling him that he was violating some rule. What a great job to have. Think about it. There are men and women at *Facebook* and all they do all day long is look for lewd photos. That's their job! Who are these *Facebook* "police?" How do I get one of these jobs?

All of the exposed skin on the dance floor and the music that night had put me in the mood, so Mark and I ended up going at it toward the end of the night.

The next time I went to a Burning Man party, I went without Mark. Just being there by myself, I attracted a lot of male attention. The best part of the Burning Man parties was the cuddle puddle. That's the name for a safe area where people go and just massage and cuddle each other. The cuddle puddle is not about sex, which is the beauty of it. I guess I wasn't hugged enough as a child, but I sure am making up for lost time. I'm definitely a Burner at heart.

The F-Buddy

(FRANK)

I should have known that this was not going to end up well. Yumi had been offering to set me up for months. Actually, the two of us had met about a year ago at this bar I frequent after work. That night, I had started a conversation with this stunning Asian woman. She was dressed in a very buttoned-up but figure-hugging suit. No, that wasn't Yumi. Yumi is, well, plain looking. Anyhow, the conversation I was having with the woman in the suit had fallen flat and it was going nowhere fast, until Yumi came along. It turned out that she knew the woman. The funny thing is that I wasn't sure if Yumi was rescuing me or her friend. Yumi took over the conversation. She just had this great sense of humor that lightened up the conversation and broke the ice. After that, I didn't see Yumi again for a few weeks.

The next time I saw her at the bar, I greeted her by saying, "Good thing you didn't bring your friend along this time. I think you'd have to rescue me from the conversation again." And, then, it just became a running joke between the two of us. I'd tease her about being friends with a woman who was such a stick in the mud. So, I started asking her when she was going to bring in a woman who was my type. She'd show up at the bar, sometimes alone or with an attractive friend or two. But when she was with her girlfriends, I never approached her, and stayed out of their conversations. I'd raise my glass or simply nod at her in acknowledgment, but never made an effort to join in on their conversations.

Then, one day she said to me, "Frank, you should give me your business card. I think I have a woman you'd like to meet." I was game. The women she came in with were always quite attractive and well put together. "I think you'd like my friend, Linny. I will give her your email address. I will be your matchmaker. I'll bill you later," she said with a wink.

"Why all the formality? Why an email? Why don't I just call her first?

Yumi whipped out her phone, held it up aiming it at me and said, "Smile! Now I have a picture of you!"

"Was that really necessary? Do you have to give her a photo of me before I even talk to her? You should just let me call the woman."

"Oh, but you can't *just* call her. You have to email her first to let her know you're going to call her."

"I have never heard of such a thing."

The next day Yumi had written me an email with Linny's email address. So, it seemed I had no choice but to play by her rules. So, I wrote Yumi back:

> From: Frank Branigan
> To: Yumi Nagoya
> Subject: Rules
>
> ====================
> Ok, I'll play by your rules, but what about sending me
> a photo of Linny? It only seems fair.
> —Frank

And then I wrote Linny:

From: Frank Branigan
To: Linny
Subject: Meeting

====================

Hi Linny,

Well it seems that Yumi thinks we should meet. Would you mind giving me your number so that I could call you to decide when to meet?

—Frank

Later that same day, Linny responded with her number and that evening I gave her a call.

"Hello is this Linny?"

"Yes, who is this?"

"It's Frank, Yumi's friend."

"Oh, right. Hi Frank."

"To be perfectly honest, Linny, I've never done anything like this before. But Yumi seemed so insistent, and I think she's a really great lady. So, tell me something about yourself. What sorts of things do you like to do?"

"Well, I'm a bit of an old-fashioned girl. I definitely expect to be picked up on a first date. A dinner and a movie is a bit cliché, but if we do go to dinner, it must be at a French restaurant, preferably on the East Side above 50th Street. I live on the Upper East Side and I believe that's where most of the best French restaurants are. And if we go see a movie, I'd like to watch a foreign film. I'm just not into tacky Hollywood movies with predictable storylines."

"You certainly are quite particular."

"Well, I do know what I like."

"I think that I could try to come up with something a bit more original than dinner and a movie," I was trying to switch gears, to get her to talk more about herself.

"If you do plan on asking me out for the weekend, I would expect you to call me before Wednesday, to make plans—preferably by Monday or Tuesday at the latest. You should call me before 9:00 P.M. and the first date should not go past 11:00 P.M."

"Thanks for laying it all out for me," I said sarcastically.

"No problem," Linny replied

"I'll call you when I have a plan," I told her and hung up, feeling a bit annoyed.

It seemed like this woman had a laundry list of requirements already and we had not even been on the first date yet! What did she expect? Did she really think she'd have me jumping through hoops for her already? What a headache, it was more trouble than it was worth.

I've had my share of bad dates with demanding women, and this was the last straw. I knew that there was one woman who'd always be happy to hear from me, so I dialed her number. The last time she'd sent me a text message at 2 A.M. I'd ignored it, but I remember what it said:

2:01 A.M. I only have one thing on my mind at this hour and you know where to find me.

I had sworn that I was going to put an end to it. That's why I'd ignored her last text message. The sex was always amazing, but outside of that, we had nothing in common. We had an arrangement that served both of us.

She answered the phone after three rings.

"What took you so long?" she asked in a breathy voice.

When I heard her voice, I wanted her all over again. She said that she was out but that she'd be right over because she'd been waiting for me. And before I knew it, there she was at my door in a long trench coat, and not much else, so I hoped.

The rest will have to be left to your imagination. As Montoya would say, I'm sworn to "shag buddy confidentiality." Oh, what the hell, what's there not to say? We did it everywhere. And I'm not just talking about that night.

She really got off on doing it in public and her enthusiasm got me excited. In alleys she would just pull up her skirt or dress and I'd slip right into that glorious pussy of hers thanks to the fact that she usually went commando or wore crotch-less pantyhose. In movie theaters, she gave me hand jobs and my fingers did a little work on her, too. There were a few blow jobs too—in the theater, on the bus, on the number 6 train going uptown, in the bathroom at a friend's party, and so many times in the back of taxicabs that I lost count. It wasn't just all about me getting serviced.

Actually, more than once, while we were in a cab, she'd unzip me, lift up her skirt and slide right on top of me. She didn't even care that we were in the middle of traffic and that people could see her bouncing up and down on my lap. This girl was hornier than all of the sailors during Fleet Week. She would do it again and again and again and didn't care who was watching.

You may have noticed that I never mentioned her name. My nickname for her was "Speedy." She could cum faster and more times than any other woman I have ever met. She was from Uruguay and used to frolic in practically nothing at Punta del Este before moving to the U.K. and becoming a flight attendant. Whenever she was in town, I was her dick of the day, or mostly the night—sometimes night and day depending on her schedule and my energy level. I am assuming she had a guy in every major international city. I just happened to be her New York guy.

Leave It on the Dance Floor

(TARA)

I was introduced to salsa dancing thanks to one of my friends, Martina, who had recently moved to New York from Venezuela. Martina was teaching beginner's salsa dance classes on Monday nights at a lounge bar in the Flatiron District and she asked me if I'd like to stop by her class and to meet up afterward. The two of us had not seen each other since college when Martina had been there as an exchange student. Since I didn't know a single step of salsa, I thought it might be a fun thing to try. That day, after my first taste of salsa dancing, I was instantly hooked.

Even when Martina stopped teaching to take a part in a Broadway play, I continued going to class every Monday night. After class, I'd linger and watch the regulars arrive. The men would step out of their street shoes, lace up their dancing shoes, and strut their stuff on the dance floor. It seemed like everyone there danced his or her troubles away. It was as if it didn't matter what had happened earlier that day when they escaped onto the dance floor.

The men would circulate around the room asking different women to dance throughout the night. There was no pretense or pick up. Everyone was there just to enjoy dancing. Quite a few of the regulars asked me to dance. The men led me around the dance floor, patiently taught me how to follow, and showed me the right steps—all while keeping time to the music.

Sal was one of the men who regularly did this. He was a bit older. I guessed that he was probably in his early fifties. But he actually looked good for his age. As I danced with Sal, sometimes I would be out of step with the music and nearly collide into another couple on the crowded dance floor. But Sal always anticipated this and managed to move us out of the way of other couples, just in time to prevent a collision. On one occasion, Sal had shielded me with his body as another couple nearly bumped into me. "Watch it," he'd said sternly as if to reprimand them. He had always been quite the gentleman, looking out for me and protecting me on the dance floor, playing the role of a Professor Higgins to my Eliza Doolittle.

In the center of the room was a round banquette and everyone used to simply throw their purses, bags, and jackets onto it. It seemed like a safe thing to do since it was in plain view and there were always people dancing around it. One night, as I was getting to ready to leave, I searched for my purse under the pile of purses and bags, but when I couldn't find it, I became frantic to the point of bursting into tears when I couldn't find it.

Sal noticed and he approached me asking, "What's wrong, Tara?"

"I can't find my purse. It's a little black clutch," I replied.

Together we dug through the pile of purses and bags and finally Sal found it for me.

"Thank goodness!" I said while drying my tears with a tissue I had taken out of my purse. "This purse was my grandmother's and it has a lot of sentimental value to me."

"Yes, it does look vintage. Well, I am glad I could help you find it," Sal responded.

"Thanks again. I've got to get going now," I said.

"Are you okay? You still seem upset. How about I walk you out?" Sal offered.

"Okay, sure," I nodded.

We talked while walking to my apartment. I was pleasantly surprised to find out that Sal was a very interesting man who had a career in women's fashion. No wonder he knew what a clutch was. Now he was doing interior design. It was the first time that Sal and I had an actual conversation. He kissed me goodnight on the cheek and asked me to have brunch with him that weekend. I didn't usually date older men. The only older man who I'd dated had been a grad student, when I was in college.

However, Sal seemed like such a gentleman. He made me feel safe and taken care of. There's something about a man who knows how to move around the dance floor especially with partner dances, I thought. It really takes skill for a man to move deliberately and purposefully, while gracefully, effortlessly guiding his partner. If he's good, a woman shouldn't even have to know how to dance. She just needs to know how to follow his lead. So, I said yes to brunch, and we exchanged numbers.

When we met for brunch on Sunday, I could see how old Sal looked in the stark light of day. Suddenly, I wasn't quite sure what I was doing there.

"Did you go for a jog today?" I asked.

"No, why do you ask?"

"Well, you are dressed in a tracksuit, which is a little unusual if you aren't running or jogging."

"I just find it comfortable," Sal responded.

Yes, it was a Sunday, but if he were out to impress me and if this was supposed to be a lunch date, the tracksuit just wasn't cutting it. His table manners also left something to be desired. He chewed loudly, smacked his lips, and spoke while he still had food in his mouth. And he didn't use a napkin once to wipe his mouth.

"Tell me about your interior design business," I asked.

"Well, actually, I'm planning to take some online courses, but I haven't registered yet. When I tried to register for the course, I found the online application confusing." Sal now had a piece of lettuce hanging off the corner of his mouth.

I pointed to the corner of my mouth and said to Sal "You have something on the corner of your mouth. You might want to wipe it off."

"Oh, thanks," he said as he wiped his mouth with the back of his hand.

I was taken aback. In real life, Sal wasn't half as smooth, sophisticated or put together as he was on the dance floor. Off the dance floor, Sal was no Professor Higgins. When Sal went to say goodbye at the end of the lunch date, he moved to kiss me on the lips. I thought about his atrocious table manners and turned my head so that he kissed my cheek instead. I decided that I would not be seeing Sal again socially, except on the dance floor. On the dance floor, Sal was a master, but in real life he wasn't.

The next time I saw Sal, it was a little awkward, but as we danced, I thought to myself, so this must be how guys feel about a woman who isn't a match for them at all, but is just good for one thing and nothing else, like an f-buddy. Just because someone has good moves on the dance floor or in the bedroom, it doesn't necessarily make for a good match. And, then, I thought, when am I ever going to find the man who is the whole package?

Cracking the Whip

(MONTOYA)

Filled with biker types in dark leather jackets, stoned out of their minds, and the types who looked like they were into having sex down and dirty, it was one of those dive bars in the city where they seemed to only serve one type of beer, in this case, Pabst Blue Ribbon. It also had a smelly, god-awful loo.

My friend, Todd, had asked me to go out with him to this bar that would make most dive bars look posh. As I stepped up to the bar, I nearly tripped over this lump on the floor. When I looked down, I saw that there was a guy encased in carpet with a sign that read: "Please make my day and step on me. Thank you." Talk about being a doormat, but I guess it was okay with him since he got off on that sort of thing.

As I looked around, I noticed there was some sort of oddball fetish theme going on with men and women dressed in black leather or shiny spandex. And as if the human doormat was not enough, I saw a picture of the devil in glowing neon lights hanging on the wall. Midgets in bikinis were dancing at one end of the bar. At the other end, men were lined up to stuff dollar bills into the G-strings of women who were crawling on top of the bar. Women in skimpy black G-strings were sliding up and down the stripper poles. It seemed like a lewd three-ring circus.

As I looked down again at the guy wrapped up in the carpet, I felt like I didn't fit in at all. Who knew that literally being a doormat could be a career? Little did I know that the show had not yet even begun.

A woman wearing some sort of a metal outfit and what looked like a chastity belt seemed to appear out of nowhere. She took what looked like a buzz saw and applied it to her chastity belt, creating sparks that shot out of her metallic pants. The crowd clapped and cheered. Next, a fire dancer shimmied around the bar, as she blew fire out of her mouth. Todd wanted to stay, but I had to get out of there. I was on my way out the door when I felt someone grab my arse.

"Excuse me!" I said turning around to see that a woman had her hand on my bottom.

"Why, did you do something that I should excuse you for? You want to apologize to me?"

She was hot. She was wearing a black G-string with black tape covering the nipples of her exposed boobs. She wore five-inch heels, heavy make-up, and fake orange and purple colored hair extensions, but I could tell she was actually pretty under all of that.

"Do you mind letting go of my arse?" I asserted.

"Your arse? Hey, limey, aren't you in the wrong neck of the woods? My name is Lilith."

"I'm Montoya."

I learned that under all that make-up she was, indeed, pretty. She had come to New York from New Mexico to make it as an actress. She was in her early twenties and had blue eyes and brown hair. To make ends meet, she was a bar-top dancer. We had sex on the first date. I made sure that I wore a condom even when she gave me a blow job and for once, I didn't try my special oral sex moves on her since I had no idea where her vadge had been. After the third date, I realized that while there was a wild intensity that attracted me to her, she wasn't exactly the girl to bring home to meet the parents.

She cursed like a sailor, and often went without her knickers. Okay, well the last thing wasn't bad, but when she went commando, she'd cross and uncross her legs exposing her vadge for anyone to see.

After I hadn't called her for a week, she started texting me continuously. I had been busy at work, so I wasn't really lying when I told her that I was busy. But it was a convenient way to avoid her and not hurt her feelings. However, Lilith was not the indirect type and she wanted to talk in person. She kept texting and leaving me voicemails, so finally, I agreed to see her.

She asked to meet at a bar on the Lower East Side. When I saw her, I decided to tell her the truth. "I really have been busy at work. But the truth is, Lilith; it just doesn't feel right between us. But we should still be friends."

"Ok Montoya, I understand, but I really just want one more for the road," she said as looked at me coquettishly. "My apartment is right next door. Let's just do it one more time. Then, I will feel better about being dumped," she said in a matter-of-fact way.

"I wouldn't say it is being dumped. I really like you and want to stay friends. I just don't see it working out long term for us."

I remembered what the sex was like with her. One thing I did know for certain was that she really knew what she was doing when it came to that. So, I took what she said at face value and I went back with her to her fourth floor walk-up for the first time. The studio apartment was weird and somewhat ominous with black walls and purple and red light bulb fixtures and an extensive whip collection prominently displayed on the walls. There was a poster of the 1973 film, *The Exorcist*, right over her bed. I moved in to kiss her after she closed the door, but she turned her head to the side and motioned me to sit on her couch.

So, I walked toward her couch but instead of joining me she locked the front door and leaned against it as if to block me from leaving.

"What are you doing?" I asked.

"You aren't leaving here. You are my prisoner and you're not leaving unless you admit that you only used me for sex," she said firmly.

"Are you out of your sodding mind?! I'm your prisoner? I thought we were coming here for sex," I said in disbelief.

"You are my prisoner!" she yelled.

"Lilith, move away from the door. This is a sick joke." I said as I stood up and walked toward the door.

She grabbed one of the many whips hanging off of the wall and cracked it right beside me, "Sit the hell down! If you try to move me out of the way, I will punch myself in the face and tell the police that you assaulted me," she said glaring at me.

I sat down and assessed the situation in my mind. I knew she was weird, but I had no idea that she was capable of this. As I sat on the couch, and looked at her without saying a word, I wondered what she'd do next.

She started screaming at me, "Taaaaaaaaaalk! Taaaaaaaaaalk! What the hell is wrong with you? Tell me you that you just used me for sex! Tell me! Tell me the truth!"

After one minute of her screaming her bloody head off, I finally realized the only way out of the room was to tell her what she wanted to hear, that I had used her. I collected my thoughts and finally said, "Lilith" in a calm voice.

But she angrily interrupted me, "Well, finally you can actually speak!"

"Lilith, you are right. I used you for sex."

She looked at me for at least two minutes without talking and barely blinking, just staring at me with piercing eyes. It was as if she were trying to pierce deep into my soul to determine if I was telling the truth.

"I have been busy at work and I need to leave now to get some sleep since I have an early meeting in the morning. So, maybe can you move from the door so I can head home now?"

"As long as you ask politely, your wish will be granted. You can leave," she responded.

"I'm sorry I hurt you. Please open the door and let me go."

She stood up and moved from the door. But as I walked toward the door, she seemed to change her mind and tried to close the door again. I pulled the door open and bolted down the four flights of stairs.

Out on the street, I looked for a cab. Lilith had chased after me and when I got in the cab, she entered the cab from the other side.

I told the driver to take me to my Upper East Side apartment. She glared at me in the cab without saying a word. I don't think she blinked once. It was like a scene out of the movie *Silence of the Lambs* except this Hannibal Lector was a female bar top dancer. As we arrived outside of my front lobby, I got out of the cab and Lilith followed me.

"Lilith, I have a doorman and he will be my witness that I didn't punch you in the face. If you follow me into the lobby, I will tell the doorman to call the police. Go home. Please. Go home," I pleaded.

"Screw you!! I don't need you!! Get the hell out of my life!!" she said as she turned and started walking down the street away from my lobby.

I walked into my lobby and went up to my apartment. Inside my apartment, I sat on my bed and kept thinking about how close I came to winding up in serious trouble. Then, I couldn't get to sleep. I should never have dated her in the first place. It's like I was looking for trouble. That's the last time my little brain does all the thinking. I've always prided myself with staying in touch with all of my exes, but not this time.

Postscript: One month later, Lilith had gotten a part on a new television series. And a year later, she had become famous. I had a laugh when I saw on *TMZ* that her manager had quit on her claiming that Lilith had locked him up in a room for a few hours. Lilith denied any knowledge of the incident.

The Four C's

(NINE)

When a woman in New York City sees a good catch, she really has to jump on him, so to speak. That was the case with Ragnar. We met at what is called "Pub Night." Several members of the Redeemer Presbyterian Church formed an unofficial bar night, emphasis on the word unofficial. The group was co-organized by my friends, David Chan and Will Chao. I've known Will for years and have always thought that he literally was one of the nicest guys on planet earth. Every month the group met at different bars.

This month the group met at Arbor Bistro in the West Village, which was partly owned by another friend of mine, Nicole Chen. Nicole was only in her twenties, but already was co-owner of this quaint and cozy restaurant. I saw Ragnar talking to a very pretty blonde woman. I got a drink and slowly walked over edging myself closer to them. Up close, I could see that he was even more handsome than I initially thought. He was about 6 foot 4 with striking good looks, an athletic physique, and a tight butt. The blonde woman was giving me a sideways glance and I could tell she wasn't happy with how I'd positioned myself so close to him.

"I really enjoyed my stay in Israel. It is God's country. You certainly feel the presence of God there in a tangible way," Ragnar said to the woman.

"I'm sorry for overhearing, but I always wanted to go to Israel. Is it really true that people feel God's presence there?" I interjected while flashing Ragnar my pearly whites.

"Most people do. There is something called 'the Jerusalem Syndrome.' Have you heard of that? Oh, I'm sorry. My name is Ragnar and this is Ashley," he said as the blonde named Ashley gave me a look, which said go away.

I held out my hand for both of them. "I'm Nine, it's a nickname. It's nice to meet both of you. So, what is this Jerusalem Syndrome?"

"Interesting nickname. The Jerusalem Syndrome happens to people all the time when they visit Jerusalem," Ragnar explained. "People feel the presence of God and many times they react emotionally to it. For me, I didn't cry, but my two friends who went with me, each burst into tears. When I asked them why, they couldn't explain it."

As we talked more about Israel, and Ashley gave me more frustrated looks, then Ragnar and I exchanged business cards. Originally from Norway, he was an investment banker, Christian, and well to do. Now, this was a real catch. I contacted him two days later and said that we should get together for a lunch on Saturday to discuss more "spiritual things." I figured that would get his attention.

We did meet for lunch at a cute little brunch place in the West Village. Over lunch as we talked, I found him even more attractive, but not only on the outside. I really wanted to see him again, so I suggested that we go to an Off-Broadway play called *The Screwtape Letters*, based on C. S. Lewis' book by the same name. He agreed and we went together. During the play, I leaned into him a few times to whisper my thoughts about the play. Ragnar commented on my perfume and started looking at me in a way that told me he was interested in me.

At the end of the night, he gave me a kiss on the cheek and asked to see me again. The next date was a kiss on the lips. The following dinner date ended with a passionate kiss goodnight. Then, sometimes we would make out in his place or mine, but we never went too far. I finally had a Christian man with integrity.

But then, Ragnar would text me to cancel our dates at the last minute. The first time he said that he had an important client in town. On another occasion, he had a late night meeting and couldn't see me. Ragnar was even more time pressed than the average corporate attorney like me. At first I took it in stride, but then I started wondering whether he was really that busy or if I was just not important enough to him to be a priority. I started second guessing myself as to whether I was being too demanding of his time or if I should be more understanding.

Our first actual fight was a month into dating. He had canceled on me yet again, at the last minute. I had bought tickets for us to attend a special not-for-profit gala. He offered to repay me for the tickets, but that wasn't the issue. The issue was me feeling unimportant and as if I was the only one trying to make the relationship work.

At a wine bistro in the Upper East Side, we met at about 11 P.M. just one hour before it was closing. "You are being unreasonable," Ragnar argued. "You do realize that I-bankers have to work long hours all the time."

"But I see you make time for other people in your life. Of course, I know that I-bankers have extremely demanding schedules, but it always seems like it is my events that you cancel on, not your friends or the events that you really want to go to. I still haven't been able to introduce you to any of my close friends," I responded.

"I will be more than happy to meet them when I have the time. But this week isn't good for me."

He had said, "This week isn't good for me" four weeks in a row. It reminded me of the Bill Murray movie, *Groundhog Day*, because he kept repeating the same excuses and it was like I was reliving the same day over and over again.

Finally, I got frustrated and said that maybe we should stop dating for a while. I thought this would make him change his priorities, but he seemed very content to hold things off with me. I guess my plan backfired since I had just offered him a way to escape. We continued texting each other and eventually the relationship ended through lack of attention, delays, and cancellations. From this, I've learned that time is a very precious commodity in New York City. It is the one resource that cannot be recovered. Once you lose it, it is gone forever.

In a short amount of time, I had started to develop feelings for Ragnar. He was an incredible catch, but it seemed like the good catch had managed to get himself out of the net. I had lost him as the old expression goes "Not with a bang, but with a whimper." I had finally found a man who had the three C's: cool, cute, and Christian, but now I realize there has to be a fourth "C," which is commitment—commitment to making our relationship a priority. Searching for the perfect man is like searching for the perfect diamond, which has to have the "Four C's."

How Big is Big?

(TARA)

Connor and I were going at it on my couch. Connor was tall, fit, and a professional soccer player. I had met Connor through Ned, who was an ex-lover of Luana. Ned was the type of person who was the life of the party, and you never knew what outrageous things he'd say. According to Luana, Ned was quite above average in size. After Ned had introduced Connor to me, he blurted out that Connor was exceptionally well endowed. He knew this because he had seen Connor in the men's locker room of their gym. If Ned thought that Connor was huge, that was really saying something. So, I was immediately curious about Connor.

I wondered just how big he was. As we stopped kissing, I looked down at his crotch. And it looked like it was about to burst, so I started unbuttoning and unzipping his pants. But before I could undo his pants, Connor reached behind my back to unhook my bra. Then, he lifted my blouse to kiss my breasts and reached up my skirt, his fingers exploring.

"Let's move it to the bedroom," I said taking Connor by the hand leading him away from the couch.

In the bedroom Connor unzipped my skirt, which dropped to the floor and then he removed his pants and boxers.

"Oh my..." I gasped. "Ned was right, you are huge! That has got to be what... ten inches?" I asked.

"Eleven inches," Connor said correcting me. "Can you guess the girth?"

"I'm afraid to guess."

"Four inches," he said with obvious pride.

"Wow. I don't think I have ever seen a specimen like that. Let me take a closer look," I said as I playfully pushed him onto the bed. I bent over and started licking his dick and tried to put it in my mouth, but gagged.

"Let me just work on the tip of it," I said and then I stopped. "Can most women fit that?"

"Don't worry. I'm sure you can handle it," Connor said reassuringly. "I will go at your pace."

Connor stopped and reached into one of the pockets of his pants and pulled out an extra large condom. He put it on and I noticed that it didn't cover his entire dick.

"Relax, lay back," Connor said as he started to go down on me. I felt his tongue filling me up and started moaning. Connor then started to move upward as he kissed my stomach, then my nipples and finally making it up to kiss my lips. He pressed himself against me indicating that he wanted to enter me. As he did this, I took a deep breath, but then the pressure was too much to bear.

"Wait! Wait!"

Connor stopped.

"I can't right now. Give me some time to get used to it. Maybe we can try again later."

We cuddled and fell asleep in each other's arms.

The next morning, I awoke. As I looked over at Connor, I saw that the sheets between his legs had formed into a tepee. I knew what that meant and feeling up to the challenge I said, "I think I'm ready now."

I reached into my nightstand for some lubricant. Connor leaned over and took the lubricant from me.

"Let me do it."

Connor started kissing me, as he tenderly rubbed my butt. Then, he moved his hands toward my inner thighs. As he felt me start to relax, he began applying the lubricant, using his fingers to prep me for what was to come. We made out for a few moments more and then he put on a condom. He started gently thrusting and the lubricant made it easier this time. I moaned with pleasure but as he started thrusting harder and deeper, I started screaming, but not out of excitement. "Wait! Slow down! That hurts!"

"Sorry," Connor said and then resumed at a slower pace going gradually harder and deeper.

"Ouch! Sorry, Connor but you keep hitting my back wall. Can you not go in all the way?"

"Okay. Why don't you get on top?" Connor suggested as he turned onto his back.

I climbed on top of him and slowly eased part of him inside of me, "Oh that's much better. Much better."

Soon I started moaning again and after a few minutes I screamed as I climaxed. But Connor didn't.

"You didn't come?" I asked afterward.

"No. I need to thrust faster and deeper."

I looked at him with some sadness. "Sorry, Connor. You're such a nice guy. But I think you're just too big for me."

That was the end of Connor. I realized that though it was good for me, and I had satisfied my curiosity, it wouldn't have been fair to continue with Connor. Sometimes you have to know when to cut the bait.

YEAR II

SUMMER

Two With One Bullet

(FRANK and MONTOYA)

Rooftop bars are a great place to be and to relax in the summertime. Montoya and Frank were having drinks at a trendy hotel rooftop bar and watching the menagerie of pretty women around them. Some wore low-slung, short skirts, revealing a flimsy thong underneath. Others wore skintight dresses devoid of panty lines, which led Montoya and Frank to wonder if some of these women were even wearing any panties at all.

Frank's Story:
"So, what do you think of what's on the menu tonight?" Montoya asked me.

"This place is filled with hoochie mamas," I said.

"Are you still sticking to your one bullet tonight?"

"Not to be sacrilegious but... many are called but few are chosen. I just need one good one," I responded.

"Are you sure about that? Just one? Maybe you should try two? Check out the trio to the right. I was checking out the tallest one when I noticed that two of them have been checking you out for the last few minutes," Montoya said.

I looked over at the three sexy women, all in short dresses revealing a lot of leg. Two were black and one was a redhead.

"Which two are checking me out?" I asked.

"The shorter of the black women and the redhead. So, let me guess, you want the shorter black woman with the big tits?"

"Without a doubt. Look at that cleavage. A man can find a lot of answers to life's questions in between those tits," I said with a smirk.

"That's like the line from that movie *Enter the Dragon*," Montoya said in response. "I'm glad you picked the one with the big tits because I was checking out the other black woman. By the way, the redhead looks like she knows a thing or two in bed. She has been checking out your crotch and sizing you up," Montoya said as he raised his eyebrows. "Either that, or she is planning to steal your wallet."

"Sure, she can put her hands in my pockets any day," I said kidding. "But given a choice, I'd take the shorter black woman."

"So, I will introduce myself to the trio, with my focus being the taller black woman and then let the other two fight over you."

I nodded. Montoya walked over and dove in by immediately engaging the trio. Five minutes later, I walked by and Montoya introduced me to the group.

"Ladies, this is my good friend Frank. Frank, this is Rosita, Barbara, and Nancy," Montoya said. "All three are nurses and I told them that you like to play doctor."

Rosita, the black woman who I was interested in, turned to me and spoke with a Haitian accent, "So, what type of doctor are you?"

"I am a gynecologist, but it is only an honorary title."

Rosita giggled in response. Barbara, the redhead, put her hand on my shoulder and said in a charming Southern accent, "So, that's great, you guys are meant for each other, Rosita here, she assists an urologist. She's seen more dicks than your average porn star."

"Really?" I grinned. "Now, that's a lot of dicks."

Barbara, the redhead, continued to introduce herself, "I assist a cardiologist. You look very fit to me. I bet your heart could take two women at the same time," she said pointing to Rosita and herself.

It was obvious that Rosita and Barbara both seemed to be interested in me, while Montoya focused on Nancy. After a few moments, I motioned to Montoya that I was leaving. As I put my hands gently behind the backs of Rosita and Barbara, it was clear that I was leaving with both of them. I hailed a cab for the three of us. Barbara had suggested that the three of us all go to her apartment in Morningside Heights.

Soon after the meter in the taxi was turned on, it seemed that we were all also turned on. I started kissing Rosita's neck and nibbling on her ear while Barbara started rubbing my crotch. All the driver could see in his rearview mirror were naked legs in the air and at one point Barbara was bouncing up and down with her blouse removed. When we reached our destination, I tipped the driver an extra 20 dollars for being a good sport and we three headed up to Barbara's apartment.

Once in the apartment, Barbara immediately started kissing Rosita very passionately. I protested that I felt left out, so Barbara told me to get undressed and to lie down on the bed. Both women took turns giving me head, but when I was about to have an orgasm they stopped.

"Not yet," Barbara said as she got on her hands and knees on the bed.

"Well you don't have to be a rocket scientist to figure out what you want," I said as I put on a condom and started having doggie style sex with Barbara. Rosita meanwhile had put her pelvis right in front of Barbara. Barbara immediately started going down on Rosita. Both women were moaning loudly and both climaxed at the same time. Then I laid down on the bed and Rosita and Barbara both started to take care of me. I wanted Rosita and told her to get on top as I put on another condom. What glorious tits she had! When Rosita came, Barbara removed my condom and resumed working on me, bringing me to orgasm.

Since the three of us had worked up quite an appetite, Barbara called for a pizza and when it arrived, the three of us relaxed in her king-size bed eating pizza together.

"This was my first time doing a threesome. I've never been with a woman before," Rosita said.

"You could've fooled me," I replied.

After we finished eating the pizza, Barbara said, "There's plenty of room in this bed, both of you are welcome to stay the night." And so we went at it a little more before we all collapsed and fell asleep.

Montoya's Story:
The next morning I woke up in bed next to Nancy. We had gone back to her place last night and I was pleasantly surprised to find that she had cooked me breakfast while I was in the shower. She had prepared some scrambled eggs, toast and instant coffee.

"Thanks so much. Being British, I am more of a tea person, but I can do coffee also," I said as I hugged Nancy from behind and kissed her on the neck. "You're a sexy sight to see in the morning. I could get used to this." I then sat down to eat the eggs and toast Nancy had prepared.

"I'll have to find out how Barbara and Rosita did with your friend last night," Nancy said as she sat down next to me and also started eating.

"Given Frank's reputation, I am sure a good time was had by all. I am positive that Frank made them both very happy."

Nancy put her hand on my dick and started rubbing it. "As happy as you made me last night?" she asked.

I smiled in response and gave Nancy a kiss on her lips. "I can't this morning. I actually have to get some work done today," I responded. "But hold that thought for tonight."

"Tonight? Would you be interested in a threesome like I'm assuming your friend Frank had? Having someone join the two of us?"

"Well, I guess it would depend on the chemistry I would have with whatever woman you had in mind to join us."

"Not a woman. I would like my husband to join us."

"Your husband?! You are married?" I said shocked by the revelation. "That is something you should have told me last night before we shagged."

"Oh, it's not a problem, my husband likes to do threesomes."

"Sorry, I don't go that way. I am only interested in women."

"Oh no, I didn't mean you and him. He likes to share me. He likes to watch or I will give him a blow job while you would do me from behind."

"I have to say a definite 'no' to that. You're great in bed, but I never get involved with married women," I said shaking my head. "And right in front of your husband, no less."

"Live a little, it will be fun. The more the merrier."

"I've done threesomes before, twice actually. But it was always with two women who weren't married. I am adventurous, but I think you just hit on something that's taboo for me. I just can't cross that line."

As I left Nancy's apartment, I gave her a kiss on the cheek and wished her well. Later, in a cab on the way to work, I thought about Nancy's offer again and was glad that I had learned something from my experience with Lilith, the hot pole dancer who had held me hostage at her apartment. I would not look for trouble anymore.

Frank's Story:

Later that same day, I called Rosita and Barbara to see if they wanted to do a threesome again. Unfortunately, my ménage a trois was short lived. I was left out in the cold when the women said that they had decided to be a twosome and not to do another threesome with me.

You Light My Fire

(TARA)

I'm always impressed when a man invites me over to his place for dinner. It doesn't happen too often, but it is a really nice gesture. I think it says a lot when a man prepares a meal and makes all this effort for you. A man probably already knows that this earns him tons of points and thinks that he'll have a good chance of having the "home field advantage" in these situations—which is probably true to a certain extent. But, if you want to know, the best place to really get to a woman is always at her place—where she is in safe familiar surroundings, completely comfortable and less likely to feel inhibited. For me, the most spectacular things that have happened in the bedroom have happened when I was at my own place; not the man's place. But, now, I am getting a little ahead of myself.

When Guy answered the door, he looked relaxed in his buttoned-down striped shirt. "Hi beautiful," he said as he leaned in to kiss me on the cheek.

We'd been on a few dates already. When we first met at Montoya's birthday party, I had noticed him immediately with his blonde hair, athletic physique, broad shoulders, and preppy style. I'll admit it; I have a soft spot for blondes. Not only was he tall, but he had the look of a male model, like one that you'd see in a Brooks Brothers catalog. At the birthday party, I'd noticed a steady stream of women approaching him all night. It was amusing to watch. I had dismissed him since he seemed a little too perfect and I wondered if he had an overblown ego from having all these women around him clamoring for his attention. I was talking to Montoya when Guy joined our conversation. As we conversed, I learned that despite his good looks, he was not the arrogant type. He was actually very down-to-earth and smart.

I'd been to his place only once before when he'd invited me over for a game night with his friends. But I'd never been to his place by myself. The vibe tonight was very different. When I walked through the door, I heard classical music playing in the background and his apartment somehow seemed soft and inviting. I noticed several candles placed around the living room highlighting the warm dark wood of his furniture. Everything looked so streamlined and modern. The last time I'd been there, I hadn't noticed all this since the room had been full of his friends sitting on folding chairs around the living room.

As I stepped into his apartment, I noticed the breath-taking view from the living room. I saw that the dining table was set with a white tablecloth, two place settings, wine glasses, and candles. I was impressed that he had clearly made an effort to create a romantic setting; however, there was no aroma of cooked food and the kitchen looked completely spic and span, so I said, "Your kitchen looks very tidy for someone who's supposedly been cooking dinner for me."

"Ah, you thought I was going to cook for you? Well, my dear, why should I cook and make a mess of my kitchen when I could order in practically anything you want? Come and take your pick. He laid out an array of takeout menus on the counter for me."

I was a little taken aback. Takeout? I mean he was actually going to just order us some takeout? But then, he seemed so sweet and charming, so I went along with it. As I looked through the menus, I saw one from a new restaurant that I'd just read about. The restaurant specialized in gourmet Chinese food, but the chef had training in the French culinary tradition. It was known for its refined dumplings and dishes. I had been looking forward to sampling the food, so we ordered some of the dishes that had been recommended in the review I'd read.

After the order was placed, Guy asked if I'd like a glass of red or white wine. Normally, I prefer red, but it was a warm summer day so I said white. He poured me a glass and suggested that we step out on the balcony to enjoy the view of the Hudson River while we waited for the food to arrive. The balcony felt like a miniature patio. On one of the walls was a huge trellis covered in ivy. A wooden bench and a big cozy wooden lounge chair with wide arms and cushy seat padding added to the ambience.

Guy motioned me toward the lounge chair. "Have a seat," he said as he sat on the bench.

It seemed obvious to me that he had put quite a bit of effort into making his balcony into a little sanctuary, so I said, "You really know how to enjoy your balcony."

"I do. It's my refuge. It's a place where I can escape to, relax, and read the paper. I had it done after I purchased this place," Guy replied.

"It also seems like you have quite the green thumb too. I have what you'd call a black thumb. I'm not good with plants. I kill them by either neglecting them or overwatering them."

The doorbell buzzer rang.

"That must be the delivery guy. Let me go buzz him in. You just sit here and relax while I get everything ready," Guy said as he got up to answer the intercom.

A few minutes later, Guy returned to the balcony and said, "Hey Tara, the food's ready. Dinner is served."

Everything was nicely displayed on a platter and serving dishes. I soon forgot that all Guy had really done, essentially, was order takeout. Sometimes, I guess, the thought or the execution and pre-sentation are what really make things count.

The food was refined and the dumpling skins thin and delicate. After dinner Guy started clearing away the plates, and as I stood up to help him, he said, "No, just make yourself comfortable. Take your glass of wine with you and have a seat on the couch."

It had been such a romantic evening and we had some nice conversation. The sexual tension had been building. So, when Guy walked out of the kitchen and over to the living room, I motioned for him to come and sit beside me. Soon, we were kissing. He started running his tongue lightly along the side of my neck as he kissed me. He looked down at the top button of my blouse and into my eyes, "May I?" he asked.

"Yes," I said.

He slowly unbuttoned the first button, then the second and the third, kissing me each time he undid each button until my blouse was completely open.

"How about adding a little bit of a different sensation to the experience?" he asked.

"Sure, what do you have in mind?" I asked.

He reached for a candle and said, "Have you ever had some hot wax dripped onto you? Lean back."

I had heard about hot wax as a form of foreplay, so I leaned back. Guy tipped the candle and let the melted wax drip off the candle onto my stomach. The warm sensation of the wax was soothing, but then I smelled something horrible. It smelled like rotten eggs. Guy abruptly put down the candle, and pulled me toward him, while reaching for a cushion, "Hold still, don't be scared," he said as he started lightly smacking the back of my head with a cushion.

"What are you doing?!" I yelled.

Guy stopped, "I'm sorry but your hair was on fire."

"What?!" I said as I touched the back of my hair and ran into the bathroom.

It looked horrible. My hair was so singed that it looked like I'd had a bad hair crimp. And just my luck, I had to go to a wedding the next day. My hair was ruined. What was I going to do on such short notice?

Guy knocked on the door, "Tara, are you okay in there? Can I come in?"

"No, this is a disaster. I have to go to my friend's wedding tomorrow and I can't go out looking this way!" What could I possibly do about this, where would I be able to find a hairdresser at this hour and on such short notice? And, then, I had an idea. "Hey, Guy, could you get my purse for me? I need to call my friend."

I heard him walk away to get my purse. A few moments later he knocked on the door, I opened it a crack. "Thanks," I said as I took my purse from him.

I called my friend Beverly, who had just gotten her certification from a dog grooming school, yes, dog grooming school. I was desperate. I knew that she'd understand and maybe she could stop by to fix this disaster.

After I hung up the phone, I felt a bit embarrassed about holing up in Guy's bathroom. So, I collected myself, took a deep breath, and stepped out of the bathroom.

As I walked into the living room, Guy stood up from the couch where he had been sitting and said, "Are you okay? I mean nothing else got burnt—right?"

"No, I'm fine. I just called my friend Beverly. She's going to come over and try to fix my hair," I said. "Coincidentally, she lives in your neighborhood."

"Oh, that's good," he said, "I'm really sorry about what happened."

"No, it's okay. I know that it was an accident. I'm sorry. I over-reacted but it's because I have to attend a wedding tomorrow. You obviously put some thought and planning into this date."

"I'm sorry that everything got ruined," said Guy.

"No, it's not your fault. I'm really kind of embarrassed, and it's about to get worse," I said.

"What do you mean?" asked Guy.

"Don't laugh, but my friend Beverly, who's on her way over, well, she is not exactly a hairdresser; she's actually a dog groomer."

"Oh, wow, really? Are you sure you want her to cut your hair?" Guy asked with a bit of skepticism.

"Well, I have no other options now. Where am I going to find a hairdresser now? And my friend's wedding is tomorrow morning in Astoria, so there's no time for me to get my haircut before then either."

"I see. In the meantime, just sit, relax, and finish your wine," Guy offered as he gestured for me to sit.

"Thanks." I sat on the far end of the couch, opposite from where Guy was standing. Then, Guy sat down at the other end and we sat in silence. Guy seemed a bit nervous and unsure of what to do. Finally, he broke the silence.

"Ummm... I really don't think it looks all that bad. You have a lot of hair. It's hardly noticeable. It'll grow back, and I bet if you pull your hair back no one would be able to notice or tell what happened."

There wasn't much he could've said or done to make me feel better or to change the situation. I knew that he was just trying to make me feel better, but the mood had been ruined.

The intercom buzzed and I felt relieved as Guy answered and I heard him tell the doorman to let Beverly come up. Soon there was a knock on the door and I leaped up off of the couch as Beverly walked in.

"The doctor's here to make a house call," Beverly said smiling and holding up her doctor's bag of tools. "You must be Guy, I'm Beverly." They shook hands.

I hugged Beverly as she said, "Don't worry I'll take care of everything. Where should we do this?" she asked Guy.

"Well, if it's going to get messy then maybe you should do it in the bathroom so it'll be a bit easier for me to clean up afterward."

So, Beverly and I went to the bathroom and she laid out her impressive array of scissors and shears on the counter. I said a little prayer and put my hair in her hands. It was like a scene right out of *Edward Scissorhands* with my hair flying everywhere and in the end, it was truly amazing what she had done. There were heaps of hair shavings on the floor. She pulled out a mirror so that I could see the back of my hair. She had evened it all out.

The day after the wedding, I decided to go see Sassy to get a proper haircut. Guy had called me to try for a second date but I want a guy who lights my fire, not one who actually lights me on fire. Some dates go so awry, and end up like a runaway train wreck, and sometimes when that happens, it's nearly impossible to get things back on track. I'm just glad that I came out of it relatively unscathed and now I've got another bad date story to tell.

Forbidden Topics

(LUANA)

Many people think I am a wild Brazilian. But I don't view myself as wild. Irreverent? Yes. Nonconformist? Yes. A Rebel? Yes. I am one of those people who doesn't want to follow the crowd. I want to be unique. I hate conformity. And if someone says something is forbidden, I ask why? If you say, "I dare you!" it makes me want to do it all the more just to show you that I can do it.

Telling me not to do something or not to say something just makes me want to do the exact opposite. I am predictably unpredictable. I am able to remain as emotionally detached as any playboy or ladies' man after having sex. I make no excuses or apologies for myself, or my actions. I am comfortable with myself and my choices in life. If you don't like me, well, that is your loss.

Of course, my dates and would-be relationships have been affected by this irreverent and nonconformist attitude. People say that in conversations you shouldn't mention politics and religion—that they are forbidden topics. I say why not? Especially when it comes to potential relationships, there should be no such thing as a forbidden topic.

If you want to be serious with someone, you have to talk about everything—sex, money matters, career goals, and also politics and religion. Women friends say I should bring it up later, once the relationship is serious, but I say find out early. Just as I want to know very early on if a man is a good lover or not, I also want to know if he is some holy roller, ultra-liberal or ultra-conservative fanatic. Why wait? I want to know from the first date.

Politically, I am an independent. I think that the two major parties need to win over the independent vote in order to win a presidential election. Thank goodness there are some people who have common sense in this country. They know that someone too far on either end of the political spectrum is not someone they want representing their concerns. The same is true of potential dates. I dated this lefty ultra-liberal once named Dan who got mad at me because I turned on Fox News one day. That relationship didn't last. I watch Fox News, MSNBC, CNN, and the BBC. I want to see different perspectives on the news. Don't tell me what channel I can watch and then expect me to still have sex with you.

But then, I also dated someone who said his entire family always voted Republican in presidential elections no matter who was running. I think that blind allegiance without paying attention to the issues is just ridiculous. I want a man who is informed on all the issues and then decides for himself who the best candidate is, or as is more common in elections, the lesser of two evils. Think for yourself. If you vote blindly, then you have no chance of taking this sexy Brazilian to bed.

On religion, I am not so much irreligious as I am just undecided. I am an agnostic. I would love to know for a fact that there is some all-powerful, caring, parental figure in the sky. But when someone tells me that they know the way to heaven, I say, "Really? Have you been to heaven? Have you seen or heard God? How can you be so sure your way is the right way?" Some people have said that they've heard a voice from heaven.

Well, I suppose that I need to see it or hear it to believe it. I would love to have God just appear to me like he did in the past to one of those prophets in The Bible. I need to see or experience some type of a miracle. It doesn't even have to be something as grand as God parting the Red Sea for me. How about making a bad lover into a good lover? That would be a miracle, or maybe that just requires hard work and patience.

I have dated people from almost every religion you can name. There was the Kabbalist who was great in bed, and the Buddhist who really knew how to use his first Chakra. Loved the Hindu guy who knew his Kama Sutra positions, and can't forget the Wiccan who did it with me naked in the woods. But the closest that I have ever come to a religious experience was whenever I'd scream, "Oh God! Oh God!" in the midst of an orgasm with my legs spread wide apart. I know, I know—it is irreverent. But it is also the truth.

Lucky, Lucky, Lucky

(ROXANNE)

I just relocated to Boston to take a position as a local news anchor. Boston is no New York and I've been adjusting to the slower pace here. But today, I had a little bit of excitement and I just had to tell someone so I wrote an email message to Tara:

From: Roxanne Shapiro
To: Tara Reynolds
Subject: Lucky, Lucky, Lucky

======================

Tara,

You're not going to believe what happened today. This afternoon I went out to run some errands in the middle of the day. Normally, I walk on Beacon Street past the Boston Commons on the way to work. As I approached one of my favorite coffee shops near the Government Center, I saw a wad of cash and several bills that had been dropped on the sidewalk. I bent down to pick up the wad and saw that the bills were actually 100 dollar bills. As I picked up the wad of cash, a woman and a man who had seen what was happening also stopped to pick up some of the other 100 dollar bills that had been dropped on the ground.

It all happened so fast that I wondered if it were a practical joke. And the reporter in me did a double take to see if it was all some sort of a set up. I looked around wondering if there were any hidden cameras around from a show like *Candid Camera* or *Punk'd* lurking around. I have no explanation for such a huge amount of money just being carelessly dropped like this on the sidewalk. But when I looked around, I didn't see anyone looking for the money that had been dropped.

The woman who had also picked up a bunch of bills looked at me and said, "Did you just see that? Someone just dropped several 100 dollar bills." I said to her, "Yeah, I looked to see if I could tell who dropped them, but I don't know." She said, "I guess someone's going be upset when they realize that they dropped so much money." And we just walked away and went about our own business.

I didn't know how much I had actually picked up, a few hundred dollars for sure. When I got home, I realized that I had picked up 800 dollars. I am still in disbelief over what happened. I mean around a couple thousand dollars total must have been dropped on the sidewalk! It was truly unbelievable. I'm not sure what to do about this, but I don't feel comfortable keeping it all. Who knows where it came from? I will definitely donate a portion of this to a good cause!

-Roxanne

Tara wrote back:

From: Tara Reynolds
To: Roxanne Shapiro
Subject: RE: Lucky, Lucky, Lucky

=======================

Roxanne,

I wouldn't worry about it, unless you hear something about any bank robberies in that part of town :-) LOL.

—T

So, I decided to donate all of the money to causes that I believe in and that took away some of the guilt. But I'm wondering why I should feel guilty in the first place. Luck is such an intangible thing. If I am lucky in my career but unlucky in love, whereas someone else is lucky in love but unlucky in his career, who is luckier?

The grass is always greener in people's minds when it comes to luck. Tara was left at an orphanage where she lived the first few years of her life. But later, she was adopted and raised by two wonderful, loving parents. On the other hand, I was raised by two neurotic parents who ended up getting divorced. So, which of the two of us was luckier with our parents?

Lucky in love is the hardest one to determine. Usually people think they are lucky to end up with the love of their life. But I think that maybe people are lucky because of the ones they let get away, meaning that they are lucky that they let the crazy ones go. Who knows? Maybe the guy who I thought was hot in the club is actually a psycho. I think being lucky depends entirely on your point of view. I saw the play *A Streetcar Named Desire* while in college. One of the lines that the main character, Stanley Kowalski, said has always stuck with me, it was, "You know what luck is? Luck is believing you're lucky."

I recently had a date with this guy who was hot. We met at an InterNations mixer. His name was Oral, of all things. Yes, as in "Oral B," the toothbrush. With a name like that, I had high hopes that this would be part of my lucky streak. He bought me a drink and we started talking. He was a computer engineer who had recently separated from his wife. Sure, I have heard that one before. Instantly, I thought, oh no, he is still technically married, but something about the way he talked about his ex made me think that he had really moved on. So, we made plans to go see a movie and then go to a restaurant on Newbury Street for dinner.

When we met, he handed me a gift basket that was wrapped in cellophane. Inside was a pink little bear with three baby blankets. I looked at it and was not sure what to say about it since it looked like a re-gifted present that someone got from a baby shower. That's not exactly what I was expecting on a first date. If anything, maybe flowers would have been more appropriate, but actually, if he had presented me with flowers that would have been too much. As it was, I had to sit through the entire movie with this baby basket next to me and then carry it to the restaurant.

At dinner, after we ordered our food, I asked Oral, "So, seriously, I've been dying to ask, what's up with this gift basket?"

"What do you mean? You don't like it?"

"It's not that, it's just that it's not your average first-date gift and frankly it looks like something you'd give to someone at a baby shower. I think you might be getting ahead of yourself here mister," I said laughing.

"Well, my wife has gotten so many of these gift baskets at her baby showers in the past, so I decided to give this one to you."

"I thought you were separated. How many kids do you have?" I asked.

"We've been separated for three months and we have six kids. My wife just keeps getting pregnant and getting separated was the only way I can stop her from having babies."

"That is why you are separated?" I asked.

"Yes, we have six children already and I didn't want there to be a seventh," Oral replied.

"Why do you have to separate then? If that is the only reason for your separation, then you still love her. Why not just wear a condom?"

"That is the woman's responsibility!" he said with a note of authority.

"Are you serious? In this day and age, why don't you just use a condom?"

"That is my woman's responsibility!!" he repeated with a lot of anger in his voice.

"No offense, but what century do you live in? Haven't you heard of birth control? You've heard of condoms?"

"I don't like your tone of voice!" he yelled.

People at other tables were looking at the two of us.

"Really, well, I don't like your caveman thinking!" I yelled and took money out of my purse to pay for my half of the bill before the food arrived. "And don't call me!" I added before I got up and left the table.

I think that luck comes in many different forms. If your jerk of a husband separates from you to keep from having a seventh kid, I'd say that you should consider yourself very lucky! I am sure there were some women at InterNations that night who thought I was lucky by having this hot guy interested in me, but guess what ladies? You were the lucky ones!

The Closure Myth

(NINE, Luana and Frank)

As Luana and I entered the Armani café on Fifth Avenue, several heads turned in our direction. Located within the multilevel Armani store was a full bar and restaurant, which attracted an upscale crowd. Luana liked to go there to check out the male models who frequented the café. In the past she had even picked up a few of them. We ordered some drinks at the bar and took a seat at a table.

"I know how busy you are, Luana. Thanks for meeting up with me. Seeing you has already lifted my spirits. If anyone would have some sound advice for me, I knew it would be you."

"No problem. I get to help you out while being able to check out the eye candy around here," Luana responded. Then, she asked me, "So is this about Ragnar?"

"Yes, it is. I am trying to get closure from Ragnar and to figure out if I could be like Montoya, and try to remain friends with my exes," I explained.

"Closure is something everyone needs or thinks they need when a relationship comes to an end," Luana responded.

"I wanted your advice because of everything you went through with Gianni. You finally moved on and I need to learn how to do that."

"Whatever advice I can give you, it's my pleasure."

"Last night I saw Ragnar at a MoMA event. He was polite but distant. I told him that I missed spending time with him and suggested that we have lunch or dinner to catch up. He said he was too busy with work."

"I know that isn't what you wanted to hear."

"You're right. So, now, I am feeling hurt again since I have spent so much time fretting about him. And after all we've been through, I think I am nothing more to him now than an acquaintance. We went out for three months! That is a long time as far as relationships in New York City go," I complained.

"So, do you really think it's still possible that the two of you could be friends?" Luana asked.

"No, I am not anywhere on his agenda. Right now I'm feeling discouraged about the whole thing. I thought I could try to get some version of closure from him, but he seems way too aloof. He just doesn't get how frustrated I still feel," I said.

"It's probably best for you to avoid him for a while," Luana advised.

"It's so disappointing that when I finally found someone who I thought was a really great catch, the problem was that he loved his career more than me. When we were dating, I knew that he needed to devote time to his career, but he didn't even call me daily or seem to miss me. One week could go by without me hearing from him, but you've heard me say this before. I think I'm rambling now."

"You're not rambling, just being human. I know you think I am the one to give you advice on this, but I think you should get a male perspective on this. You should ask Frank," Luana suggested.

"Frank? Not Montoya?"

"Not for this situation. Frank would be better at ending relationships than Montoya. Frank is the guy to talk to."

"Really?" I asked.

"Frank will be able to get into Ragnar's head better than Montoya or myself. Trust me," Luana said confidently.

Later that week, I met up with Frank for a bite to eat at a little Japanese restaurant in Midtown East. I told Frank about the last time I had bumped into Ragnar to see what he would have to say about it.

"Don't let other people bog you down with their bull crap! This guy sounds like he has moved on and I believe you should also. He isn't worth it," Frank said after taking a swig of his beer.

"So, I shouldn't try to stay friends with him?" I asked, curious to hear Frank's reasoning behind this.

"Sometimes it is hard to be friends with someone you once dated. Maybe he is thinking you want to start up the romance again and is distancing himself," Frank responded. "You know I care about you, Nine. You need to shrug this guy off and soon you will be back in the saddle again."

"You think so?"

"I know so," Frank said with conviction in his own opinion. "It is a waste of time to brood over him. You need to stop agonizing over this. Maybe, one day you can be friends with him, but not right now."

"I've already stopped calling him and emailing him," I said.

"That's good. Remember, it's his loss!"

"I know. The book is definitely closed. But I might bump into him at a pub night event organized by David Chan and Will Chao. Will is a mutual friend of both of us and I don't want to cause a scene at one of his events," I said worrying aloud.

"If you bump into him at a party, there is no need for a scene, a fight, or even any contact at all," Frank advised.

"You mean, I shouldn't even give him a hug?" I asked.

"Why do you feel the need to give him a hug? But if he goes to hug or kiss you, then respond. But never—and I mean never—be the initiator. Right now, you should avoid him and he will soon realize what he is missing. You also need to think about why you are doing or not doing something. In other words, none of it should be a ploy to get him back. Sometimes we don't realize that's our motivation behind things, especially when we are still not really over someone yet."

"But I don't want to do something that will hurt him," I explained.

"Don't worry about hurting his feelings, clearly he's not thinking about yours. You need to think about yourself first and to protect your own heart. Getting closure or the need for closure from someone else is a myth. You need to come to terms with it on your own. Now, that is easier said than done. I speak from experience. Remember, you are the only one who can give yourself closure when it comes to Ragnar."

"Thanks so much Frank. Would it be okay if I be the initiator now and ask you for a hug and kiss?" I asked teasing him.

"That is the best idea you've had all night," Frank responded teasing me back.

I gave Frank a big bear hug and kissed him on his cheek.

Postscript: The next time I saw Ragnar at a party, I started to walk toward him to greet him, but then I thought about what Frank had said and stopped myself. Instead, I went to get a drink and started talking to other people at the party. I didn't initiate any contact with him. He looked at me across the room several times during the party, trying to make eye contact. I never met his eyes as I continued talking to other people. Finally, I decided to leave the party early without greeting Ragnar. Later that night, I felt a pang of sadness in my heart for what might have been, but I knew it was better this way.

Falling Too Hard Too Fast

(TARA)

I was back in the hair salon with Sassy for a haircut. As Sassy combed through my hair, I asked, "So, how's it going with your guy?"

"Oh, it is going so well! I think he is a keeper. We have been inseparable. And, he's still as attentive as ever. I think we are going to move in together! What about you? You seem to be quite pleased about something," Sassy said cheerily.

Sassy was right. It was uncanny how she could sense how I felt about the man I was dating at the time.

"Well, I don't normally do this, but I just slept with someone who I had a drink with the other night!" I confessed. I had not told any of my friends about this recent development, but Sassy was not in my immediate circle of friends, so it was safe to tell her.

"Oh! Who is he? How did you meet? Do you see any potential?" Sassy asked.

"Actually, he is someone who I have known for years. We have always had this flirtation but never acted on it. We have a lot of friends in common. He was in town this weekend for a visit from Hong Kong," I explained.

"I see, so now what?"

"Well, uhm it kind of just happened and afterward he told me that he's in a relationship with someone, but he knows that she is not the one."

What I didn't explain is that I had spent the entire weekend with Reid. Our coupling felt so natural, as did his holding my hand as we walked to brunch the morning after. As we ate and talked about what each of us was looking for in a relationship and about our past relationships, he reached for my hand several times and looked deeply into my eyes. I felt as though we had both bared each other's souls and that what we had experienced was not just a tryst in the bedroom.

He told me very frankly about his relationship situation. The woman he was involved with was from a very well-connected family in Hong Kong. They had been living together for a while now. Their lives were so intertwined, but he felt that she was not "the one." Then, he had asked me how I felt about him already being in a relationship with someone else. I didn't know what to say or if I had the right to say anything.

On the last day that we were together, Reid told me that if I ever needed anything, I could always go to him, even though he was going back to Hong Kong. He told me that he came to New York several times a year on business and I actually started to consider for a moment whether I could become involved with him. After all these years, we had finally ended up in bed together and things seemed to just fall into place. I had not told anyone about this. It was best to keep it a secret, especially since he was already involved with someone else. Reid and I also had many friends in common, and if news of our tryst ever got out, the rumors would have spread like wildfire.

Sassy stopped cutting my hair, "Hey, you should have fun, nothing wrong with that, but be careful with this guy. I don't think you should be getting your hopes up. I don't like how this sounds."

As Sassy blow-dried my hair, I thought about what she had said.

A few days later, I hadn't heard from Reid. I knew that he had several business meetings lined up during the week. He mentioned that was the purpose of his trip. I also knew what day he was leaving to return to Hong Kong. Somehow, a part of me still hoped to hear from him or to say goodbye in person. I felt conflicted because deep down, a part of me wanted him, but I also knew that it could never be. On the day that Reid was to leave, he didn't call or text. I cried that night because I knew that I had no right to miss him as much as I did at that moment. So, I sent him one last text message, which said:

> 9:57 P.M. Thanks for being so real and open with me in the time that we were together. Now I will miss you more than I probably should.

I cried because I knew that I would miss him, not just because I knew he was leaving, but because I had already decided that despite it all, I could not and would not be second best. I would not get involved any further, because if I did, that's what I would be, second best. I did not want to take someone else's leftovers.

Ultimately, I knew that I would not be able to bear sharing him with anyone else. It would just tear me apart to be stuck in a waiting game or wondering where his affections were and playing by his rules. Better to suffer the pain of loss now I thought—rather than enduring what would probably have been a long, drawn out, and emotionally draining affair.

And I knew that I wouldn't want to be in the other woman's shoes. I wouldn't want to have someone doing that to me. It was the greatest amount of heartache that I had ever felt in such a short period of time. I had never fallen for someone so hard, so fast.

The Men's Room

(NINE and Frank)

I love to go out dancing at the clubs on the Lower East Side and in East Village. These clubs are not too pretentious with the velvet-rope attitude of those in the Meatpacking District. A great night out for me would be dancing and flirting with guys, which sometimes led to kissing or making out, but that's usually as far as it went, it didn't lead anywhere else.

That's kind of how I met Randy, in Atlanta, on a different sort of dance floor. I was there for a friend's wedding. She was a friend from church and she loved dancing just as much as I did. So, I knew that her wedding would involve a lot of dancing, which would provide a great opportunity to meet some cute Christian guys.

Dancing always seems to loosen people up and people who don't normally dance often end up getting lured to the dance floor at weddings. At the wedding reception, there were plenty of good-looking guys. And sure enough, when I was on the dance floor, a good-looking guy came up to me, introduced himself, and started dancing with me. He had some pretty good moves. After a few songs, we decided to take a break, so we sat down at a table and drank some champagne.

"So, Nine is an unusual name, isn't it?" Randy asked.

"It's a nickname, but I hear that Randy is a very common name here in the south," I responded.

"That is true, but I like to think that I am an uncommon man."

"Well, I guess, time will tell."

"Funny, that you say that. I am moving to New York City in two weeks. I've accepted a position at a major architectural firm there. So, can I look you up when I move there?"

"Of course," I said in disbelief at my good fortune.

Randy was a graduate of Emory and spoke with the cutest southern accent. On the first date, he told me that he was having major reservations about being a Christian. He had many problems with The Bible. He said that he just didn't believe in all of the miracles in The Bible. But he had a Christian upbringing and considered himself a Christian.

That was something that I could work with. I would help him come around. At least that was my mindset. After the first date, I was already swooning for him. Aside from his good looks, I fell in love with his brain. This guy was super smart and I had always wanted a clever and witty guy. We started dating immediately. I am sorry to say that I gave in to his pressure and started giving him blow jobs. He seemed content with the blow jobs and didn't mind that I didn't want to have intercourse with him. I would soon find out why.

We'd been dating for about a month when we went to an Italian restaurant in Tribeca and clubbing afterward. We danced for about twenty minutes and then Randy had to go to the men's room. He took a long time before he finally returned.

"That took a long time. Are you okay?" I asked when he returned.

"I'm fine. The veal parmigiana I just had didn't agree with my stomach. But I am fine now," Randy responded.

We went to a dark corner and made out for a while, but, then, I got thirsty so Randy went to the bar to get me a drink. The bar was crowded, so it took him about fifteen minutes to get back to me. While he was gone, I saw Frank walk by.

"Hey Frank!" I called out. Frank turned and came to where I was and gave me a little hug and a kiss on the cheek.

"Hi Nine, you here by yourself or out on a date?" Frank asked.

"My boyfriend is getting us a drink at the bar."

"Boyfriend, huh. How come we haven't heard about him yet? Point him out to me."

"He's the slim guy wearing the gray shirt and dark jeans," I said.

"You mean the guy handing over his credit card to the bartender?" Frank asked with an odd tone to his voice.

"Yes," I responded.

"Oh…" Frank said again with an odd tone to his voice.

"I know you Frank. Why the 'Oh'?"

"I don't think I should say," Frank said hesitantly.

"It's okay. Whatever it is, you can tell me. I would rather know than not know," I insisted.

"I was in the men's room about twenty minutes ago, and in these clubs you can see everything. I've even made out myself with some chicks in the men's room from time to time. But when I was in there, I saw the guy you just pointed out getting a blow job from another guy."

"No way!" I said raising my voice at Frank in reaction. The club was noisy, but clearly that wasn't the reason I'd raised my voice.

"Listen Nine, don't shoot the messenger. You asked and you said you would rather know, than not know," Frank said with a serious tone in his voice.

"You're right. I did say that. I apologize for raising my voice," I looked over and saw Randy, who was walking back from the bar with drinks for us. "He is coming back now with the drinks. Frank, please let me handle this solo."

"Sure thing," Frank said as he left.

"Who was that?' Randy asked as he handed me my drink.

"A friend of mine. So, how is your stomach now?"

"It's fine."

"My friend who just left told me that he saw you in the men's room earlier."

"What did he say?" Randy asked.

"That is an interesting question. Why would he say anything?" I asked with a tone of anger.

"He saw something?" Randy asked.

"Oh, my God! It's true! Why?" I demanded.

"It didn't mean anything," Randy insisted.

"With a guy? You can't even cheat on me with a woman?" I said exasperated.

"I just met him in the men's room. It didn't mean anything."

"Well, did all those blow jobs I gave you mean anything at all to you?"

I stormed out of the club with Randy following me. I hailed a cab, quickly got in, slammed the door, and left Randy standing on the corner.

He immediately tried calling and texting me, but I ignored him and deleted all his contact information. After that, I vowed I would never give in to a guy's sexual demands again. I would remain pure.

Every Woman is Different

(MONTOYA)

I had the window seat on a flight to D.C. for a business trip. Next to me was a sexy, dark-skinned woman wearing a very short skirt. She looked Dominican or maybe Mexican. Her legs were absolutely fantastic. Although I was interested in starting a conversation with her, I hadn't had much sleep the night before due to some late night shagging.

I closed my eyes for just a few minutes and went into that half-awake, half-asleep state that you sometimes find yourself in on a flight. As I closed my eyes, I started fantasizing about going down on the woman next to me and then my thoughts turned to the vast array of women who I have done that to in the past. I have to say that I am not as expert at giving oral sex to women, like let's say a lesbian porn star would be, but I do consider myself a very talented and experienced amateur.

Although the women I have been with have definitely appreciated my shagging skills, my oral skills seemed to really impress them. That tells me that most guys probably just don't know how to do it right. I have heard so many women moan or scream my name: "Montoya! Montoya!" As I see it, I have pleasured quite a few women of many different tastes and sounds over the years. My thoughts drifted off to the many different women I've been with over the years.

Kimora moaning, Wanda screaming, Roberta moaning, Janet screaming, Yan moaning, Jean panting, Pamela screaming... Coughing up the hair out of my mouth after doing Tandy. Desiree screaming, Shannon moaning, Jessica arching her back while she lay upside down, Barbara screaming so loud she hurt my ears, Meghan moaning... Trying to find my way through Maxine's massive forest of hair... Jennifer moaning, Nadine screaming... Pouring whipped cream on Tamara, Katie moaning... Pouring chocolate on Chelsea... Ellen screaming. Patty sitting on my face as she rocked back and forth. There have been women of every cup size, hairy and shaved, cougars and barely legal.

With the many women I've been with, there are definitely two who really stand out in my mind.

Nanette was a beautiful redhead with huge D-cup tits and the best-feeling skin ever. When we ended up in my apartment together for the first time, I pulled off her panties exposing a full bush of red hair. When I went inside her, there was no response, absolutely nothing. No moaning, no screaming, nothing! I felt like I was making love to a beautiful corpse. My fingers and oral sex skills didn't work either. I felt like she needed Gene Simmons' tongue to get her excited. It was the only time a woman ever made me feel as if my equipment was inadequate.

The second most memorable was a beautiful Greek woman, Melina, who I called my Greek goddess. She was the best tasting woman I've ever had. No woman ever got more wet or tasted so good. I would have her taste in my mouth for an entire day after, even after brushing my teeth and gargling with mouthwash. She was the best dessert that I have ever had, even better than green tea ice cream, which is now one of my favorite desserts.

And that wasn't the best part—she often had multiple orgasms. She was unstoppable. My all-time record with her was seventeen times over the course of a night and the next morning. After that, my ears hurt for a day afterward because each time she came, she'd arch her back and squeeze her legs, with my poor head in between. What strength she had in those legs when she climaxed! The first time I ever performed oral sex on her, the neighbors pounded on the walls since she screamed so loudly. I was afraid the neighbors would call the police and hushed her. When she offered to tie her scarf over her mouth, it just seemed to excite her even more. She lived in Greece and would only visit New York once a year so we'd have an annual shag-buddy fest.

"Every woman is different," I whispered out aloud without thinking in my half-asleep state. The woman next to me asked if I was talking to her and the next thing I knew we were talking and flirting with each other the entire flight. Her name was Lucinda and she was from the Dominican Republic. She turned out to be a screamer and had a totally shaved vadge. Lucinda was so skilled at giving oral sex that the blow job she gave me made me almost want to scream myself.

YEAR II

FALL

Slut by Association

(NINE, Luana and Montoya)

I met Chad, a very fine, attractive black man at an NAACP fund-raiser. He was born and bred in Oklahoma, and thank God, he was a Christian. He also had old-fashioned, good manners. After we had gone on a few dates and finally kissed, he didn't even try to make out with me. He seemed perfect, and I thought, this is a guy I can introduce to my friends. So, I invited him to a party that Luana was hosting at her apartment. She often had small parties for about forty people with space for twenty-five people in her living room and fifteen people on her outside terrace. At the door Luana greeted us.

"So, this is Chad? Pleasure to meet you," Luana said.

When I went for a glass of pinot noir, Chad gave me a look. He got himself a glass of soda. I realized that Chad had never seen me drink alcohol before. Later in the night, Luana turned down the lights and everyone started dancing, everyone but Chad. I tried to coax him to give it a try, but he just sat on the sofa and watched me dance with Montoya. Montoya and I went into the kitchen and Chad followed us. Montoya offered to pour me another glass of wine.

"Chad, you really have a great woman there, with Nine. Many men are jealous of you," Montoya said.

"What about you? Any girlfriend?" Chad responded.

"That would be a miracle. Montoya is a real playboy. I can't keep up with how many women he's been with," I kidded.

Luana had walked into the kitchen and heard what I'd said.

"I don't know, Montoya, I wonder if you have been with as many women, as I have been with men," Luana said laughing.

"I don't know, but I think if we added our numbers up, we would need a mathematical genius to do the math," Montoya responded.

Montoya, Luana, and I were all laughing, but Chad wasn't laughing.

As we left the party and walked out of Luana's apartment building, Chad was visibly angry.

"You seem upset. What is it?" I asked.

"I thought you were a Christian," Chad said.

"What kind of question is that? You have gone to church with me," I replied somewhat annoyed.

"But you have sluts and playboys as your friends."

"Are you talking about Luana and Montoya? Luana is a very nice woman once you get to know her and Montoya is my closest friend in New York. He is the best guy I've ever met," I said defensively.

"I was taught not to be unequally yoked with unbelievers," Chad insisted. "You lie down with dogs, you will wake up with fleas. By befriending sluts, you become a slut yourself."

"Did you just call me a slut? Are you serious? I am not 'lying down with dogs.' I've met so many non-Christians who are more moral and generous of spirit than the average Christian."

"And you drink alcohol," Chad said shaking his head in disapproval.

"I had two glasses of wine! That's social drinking. I'm not drunk or even tipsy," I said raising my voice.

"To me, The Bible is very clear on many issues. You also dance."

"Yes, I do. I dance, I drink, and I have a playboy as a best friend. So, in your book do you think that means I am as big a slut as you think Luana is?!" I yelled.

Chad didn't say anything. He just looked down at the ground as we walked.

"I am a Christian. I pray and read The Bible every day. I go to church every Sunday. I lead a growth group. To me, everything isn't always black and white. Thomas was one of the apostles and he had his doubts; but that didn't disqualify him from being an apostle. The only one who has to approve of my Christian lifestyle is God."

Chad still didn't respond.

"If you don't mind, I will head home by myself from this point on," I insisted.

I held out my hand and shook Chad's hand as a goodbye.

Chad was a fundamentalist but without the "fun" in fundamentalist. To him, I was a slut by association, therefore, not a good Christian. Then there was Randy, who I thought was a slut when I discovered that he had gotten a blow job from a man he hardly knew in a public restroom. I guess what is shocking to a person is all in the eye of the beholder.

Try It, You Might Like It

(KATIA)

While at the Princeton Club for an All-Ivy event, I noticed a very good-looking man who was surrounded by several women. It was a black tie event and many of the women looked older than he was. I went to get a glass of champagne and moved closer to where he would be able to get a better look at me. He was really sexy, with dark hair and a ruggedly masculine toned athletic build. When he looked over I turned to give him a full view of me. Then I leaned over as I put some pate on a cracker because I knew that would accentuate my cleavage, which was exposed by the plunging neckline of my evening gown. He seemed to stop in mid sentence as he looked across the room mesmerized by my breasts. He excused himself from the women surrounding him and started walking straight toward me.

"You seem to be Mr. Popularity tonight," I said to him as he stood beside me and reached for a piece of cheese.

"Yes, I am a regular at these All-Ivy events, so I've met several of the ladies here before," he said looking down at my chest. "But you, I definitely would have remembered," he said with a charming accent as he continued staring straight at my chest.

"I'm glad you appreciate the view, but many men say my face is worth looking at also," I said laughing slightly.

"Oh! Pardon me! I didn't even realize I was doing that," he said somewhat embarrassed and now looked up at my face.

"No problem. I have come to accept that my girls get all the attention," I said in amusement.

As we talked I found out that he was originally from Australia and worked in Manhattan as a commercial real estate agent. He was the totally athletic type. He had run a few marathons and done a few triathlons. And every year he also rode in the Tri-Borough Bike Tour. Obviously, he was in great shape and very outdoorsy, and he was really sexy. Oh, did I say that already? But I thought, what would we ever have in common? He had some money but it didn't seem like he had made it to the top rung of the ladder in his field. He seemed too laid back and not as ambitious as the men I've usually dated.

He suggested a picnic in Central Park as our first date. I guess the look on my face told him that wasn't such a good suggestion. I am not exactly the outdoorsy type. So his second suggestion was to take me to a Broadway show. Now that was better, the man was already learning.

At the expensive Japanese sushi restaurant he took me to after the show, he said, "Now Katia, as you know, I am very proud Aussie and an outdoors man at heart. Let's do a picnic in the park as our next date."

"Darling, I really don't like the idea of having a date in the dirt," I responded.

"Just try it. How about you pick the place one time and then I pick the venue the next time. We can alternate."

I thought to myself, God! This is one of those men who believe in a 50/50 relationship. I am going to have to wean him off that right after we have sex.

We made out a little in front of my apartment building as he had walked me home that night, and then he got in a cab. The next day

Cameron called and again he insisted on taking me to a picnic in Central Park the following weekend.

"Have you ever had Aussie food?" Cameron asked on the phone call. "Don't worry, I won't prepare anything too out there like bush tucker. And I promise there won't be any kangaroo or crocodile."

"What's tucker?" I asked wondering if this was some Australian term that I hadn't heard of before.

"Bush tucker or bush food. I guess I really need to educate you about Australian food. Bush food is what the Australian aborigines would eat, like indigenous plants, nuts and berries, and sometimes witchetty grubs," Cameron explained.

I felt like I could feel him smiling on the other end of the phone. I didn't know whether to take what he said seriously or not, but I found myself reacting to what he said. "Grubs?! You mean like worms," I said cringing.

"I'm just pulling your leg; I promise there won't be any of that. Besides I can't easily get my hands on those things since they are all indigenous to Australia. I'll take care of everything, you won't need to lift a finger, just show up!" Cameron said enthusiastically.

I half wondered if we had been in Australia instead of New York City, would he have really tried to introduce me to some of this odd sounding Australian food? He was really sexy and I wanted to see him again, so I thought, let me get this out of the way and then I can educate him as to how he should really treat a lady.

The following Saturday Cameron and I were supposed to meet at the entrance of Central Park West and 65th Street. We were going to have our picnic in Sheep Meadow. As I approached 65th Street I recognized his muscular silhouette from a distance. He spotted me and waved.

"Hi Katia! It's so nice to see you again," Cameron said as he gave me a sensuous kiss on the lips. He was carrying a backpack and dressed in a green Billabong T-shirt and khaki pants. I could definitely picture him surfing back in Australia. I was also dressed casually in a red, wide scoop-necked top and skinny black jeans, but in a way that highlighted my best assets, of course.

"Thanks, it's nice to see you too."

We walked into Sheep Meadow and found a spot under a tree. Cameron pulled a blanket from his backpack and laid it down for us to sit on. Then, he started laying out plates, on which he placed an assortment of fruit, vegetable sticks, crackers, and toast. He also pulled out a few jars of different spreads, plastic utensils, and cups.

"Did you actually prepare all of this yourself?" I asked trying to be polite, but thinking that he shouldn't have wasted his time and could have just gotten it catered.

"Would you like something to drink? How about some sparkling water? I have raspberry flavored and lemon/lime."

"I'll take some of the raspberry," I said as Cameron poured some into a cup and handed it to me.

"Are you ready to try some Aussie food?"

"Sure."

"This is an Aussie favorite. It's as Australian as peanut butter is American," Cameron said as he held up a dark colored jar with a yellow label and lid.

"Oh, I've never had that. What is it?"

"It's called vegemite. Just put some of it on a piece of toast," Cameron said opening the jar.

"Can I see the jar? Is it some sort of a vegetarian thing?" I asked him.

He handed me the jar. I took a spoon, scooped a bit out of the jar and put it in my mouth to taste.

"Oh no, that's not how you eat it!" Cameron exclaimed.

I soon discovered why he said that. It was extremely salty, and didn't taste like peanut butter at all! I almost wanted to spit it out, but figured that wouldn't be too ladylike to do that, so I reached for my cup and took a few gulps of sparkling raspberry juice to wash it down.

"You need to put it on thinly, on a piece of toast. This is how you make it, first put some margarine on a piece of toast and then put a thin layer of vegemite on top," Cameron said demonstrating. He made one for himself and one for me. "Here try it and let me know what you think."

But it was too late. I had no desire to have any more of it. "No thanks, I think I'll pass," I said. "What is that stuff made of?"

"It's made of fermented yeast," Cameron explained.

"That doesn't sound too appetizing. Yeast is only good for two things. Making beer and bread."

"Well it is basically a byproduct of the beer making process."

"Knowing that doesn't exactly make me want to try it again," I said helping myself to some grapes.

"Come on you haven't even tried it properly." Cameron bit into a piece of his toast and continued, "Are you sure you don't want to try a piece of this, just take a little bite?"

"No that stuff is vile and it smells nasty too."

"I'm wounded. Don't you know that you should never say that to an Aussie?" Cameron said.

"I feel like it's like bad medicine. It tastes so horrible. It's like what doesn't kill you makes you stronger. Except that with medicine you endure it because you know it's good for you, but I don't think that vegemite is going to be curing me of anything."

The date went downhill from there. We tried to have some polite conversation and Cameron tried to get me to try the vegemite a few more times. I made a few sarcastic comments in response as a joke.

Then he told me that his idea of a romantic getaway was to spend a weekend roughing it out in nature, sleeping under the stars, without modern conveniences like running water or electricity.

He thought that getting back to basics would be a good test of character and compatibility. I suppose it would be something to able to tolerate someone else's "au naturel" scent after a few days of not showering, but that's not a test that I want to be put through. I want to stay in a five star hotel, not a tent in the middle of nowhere. I knew I wouldn't be able change him enough to suit me. So even though most women would think I was crazy for letting this hunk of a man get away, I decided not to see him again after the picnic. I would rather be with someone who wants to feed me champagne and caviar, not witchetty grubs.

A Smile on the Subway

(TARA)

At the end of another long day at work, I was sitting on the train on the way home, feeling exhausted. I slumped in my seat and turned on my iPod. I closed my eyes and for a moment I was in my own little world. After graduating from Columbia with an MBA in Finance, I'd landed this position as CFO and at first it was exciting. I'd been groomed for a position exactly like this, and it might sound a bit nerdy, but focusing on strategic financial planning and building robust revenue streams was quite rewarding. I knew that my work had a direct impact on the company's growth and survival.

But now, the job had become more about budgeting, cost cutting and the bottom line since the recession. Lately, I'd been feeling kind of depressed about work because there were a lot of tough decisions that had to be made, which meant layoffs. Some really good, competent people would have to be let go as divisions were merged or phased out.

My iPod was running out of battery power, so I turned it off and removed the earbuds. I looked up and saw a guy standing a few feet away. He looked at me and smiled gently. Something about the way that he was dressed seemed very European. He widened his smile as he held apart his index finger and thumb at the corners of his mouth, gesturing that I should smile. I couldn't help but smile back. I guess I must have looked kind of serious or depressed. As the train approached my stop, I got up and walked toward the door and he did too.

"Hi. I'm Sebastian," he said to me as we walked up the stairs out of the subway station. "Looks like you could use a friend. Can I buy you a cup of coffee? There's a great little cafe just around the corner that my friend opened up called 'Roasted.' "

I knew the place. It was a cute place. It wasn't just another one of those franchised coffee chains.

"What do you have to lose?" He continued, "If you're not rushing off to be somewhere right now that is. It's my treat." I detected a hint of a French accent, and I've always been a bit partial to foreign accents, especially European ones.

"Oh, you know the owner, do you? And what line of business are you in?"

"I'm a coffee exporter. Come, I'll introduce you to the owner. She has a great story about how she started her own business. It's inspiring."

"Okay," I found myself saying. Why not? I thought. Frankly, while he did have a charming French accent, I was more interested in meeting his friend than anything else. A woman who owned and ran her own business, this was impressive. Maybe it would give me inspiration, especially since I was starting to have doubts about my chosen career path.

It turned out that the owner of Roasted, Grace, had made it her mission to make coffee into an art form and to merge the enjoyment of coffee and art. She had been a banker but when she got laid off, she realized that the only job security she could be sure of was from a job that she created for herself. At Roasted, every cup of latte was presented as a foamy, floating work of art. The foam of each cup was groomed into the image of a leaf, a flower, a heart, a bird, or some other whimsical, artistic creation.

In keeping with this artistic flair, her coffee shop was also a show-case for art, a sort of mini gallery. Paintings or photographs by local artists hung on the walls and were available for sale. Every few months, the "exhibits" would change. Each time a new exhibit was installed, she hosted an art opening party at the coffee shop for the artists whose works of art would be gracing the walls for the next few months. It was amazing to hear how she had decided to start all over and to reinvent herself.

As for Sebastian, he just had this way of making me feel at ease. He had grown up in a small town in the French Basque region, so he spoke French and Spanish and probably a handful of different languages as most Europeans do. He wasn't at all pretentious or snooty as many of the French are too often labeled, but then again, he was not from the big city, meaning Paris. I think that people from major cities all around the world—from New York City to Shanghai—often get a bad rap for being tough, hardened souls. But I think, it's because big city people usually have their guard up by default, to shield themselves from the unwanted or unsolicited encounters of questionable people.

I found Sebastian to be a fascinating man. Our backgrounds were worlds apart, but we could talk for hours. He was so different from most of the men who I'd dated, who've mostly been American. Maybe it was because of our dissimilar backgrounds that we had so much to talk about. Besides, the easy rapport that we had, he was, in a word—smoldering. There was something about the way he looked at me and all the little French pet names that he had for me—"mon amour," "ma belle," "cherie"—that just made me feel so sexy.

Our lovemaking sessions were exactly that—they were tender expressions of love. With Sebastian, I never felt rushed. Neither of us was really a morning person, so, on the weekends, we would often sleep-in lying cocooned in bed with our bodies intertwined, in a sort of prolonged foreplay in a dreamlike state, that kept me feeling aroused, ready, and longing for the next round, which could happen at any moment.

It may sound like the sex was getting comfortable, but for me, I would definitely say that was not a bad thing in my book. In fact, for me, once I really started to feel comfortable and relaxed, that was when things would start to get really interesting.

The coffee shop became our place. We'd often meet there and wander down into the West Village afterward. I learned how he had built his business. He was a successful entrepreneur and very smart with his money. Things were so relaxed and unhurried with him. For the first time in a long time, I realized that I was not anxious or in a rush to define things, as I had been in past relationships. I just took things day by day, and I was really in the moment with him. For once, everything was cruising along smoothly.

Madison Avenue Candy

(FRANK)

I learned a long time ago that "clothes make the man." I favor Armani suits and Italian shoes. So, I went for a stroll along Madison Avenue to see if I could find some nice new dress shirts. I was looking through the window of a men's haberdashery, when a pair of shapely legs caught my eye.

As I peered inside the store, I saw a very attractive woman with thick, long, layered blonde hair. She had a fair complexion; her hair was like the mane of a lion, giving her a rather wild look but everything else about her was classic Madison Avenue chic.

I entered the haberdashery and casually looked at a few shirts. As I held one shirt up to look at it, I stole a look and saw her face more closely. Up close she was not only very attractive but actually a real beauty with striking hazel eyes. She looked about twenty-five years old at most.

As our eyes met I asked, "What do you think of this shirt?"

"Nice, it seems to suit you," she replied.

"Really, why do you say that?"

"I could totally see you as picking up some young thing dressed in that shirt," she said knowingly.

"Do I seem like a player to you?"

"Definitely," she said. "I'm sure you could tell me stories about how many women you've picked up recently, but I need to get going and get myself a chocolate fix. Excuse me."

She turned toward the cash register to purchase a tie that she held in her hand. A light bulb went on in my head, so I quickly walked out of the store and went to the newsstand on the corner. I got back in less than two minutes to present her with three types of chocolate bars, one milk chocolate, one dark chocolate, and one with almonds.

"Wow!" she said as I handed them to her.

"I didn't know which type of chocolate you would like, so I got you a few to choose from."

She seemed touched by my gesture of thoughtfulness and waited for me, eating the chocolate with almonds as I purchased the dress shirt and asked to have it monogrammed. It was nearly 5 P.M. and since she was hungry, I suggested we have a bite to eat at the nearby Bemelman's Bar of the Carlyle Hotel. We ordered some appetizers. Then, she ordered a Long Island Iced Tea, which she seemed to practically inhale in three large gulps.

After that, she got a second Long Island Iced Tea, then another and finally a fourth one. As we were drinking and eating, I found out that her name was Catherine but that her nickname was "Candy." We laughed about how we were meant for each other—me getting her chocolates and her nickname being "Candy."

I found out that she was from one of the wealthiest families in New York. She would spend most of her days shopping on Madison Avenue or Prince Street or hanging out at the Core Club or at SoHo House. Daniel on Madison Avenue was her favorite restaurant and she freely professed that she loved La Perla because of how it made her feel—sexy. By her fourth Long Island Iced Tea, she was slurring her words. We had been at the bar talking for nearly three hours. She went to the ladies room at some point, and when she came back, she first put her hand on my leg, and then a few moments later she put it right on my dick and rubbed it gently with her index finger.

"Take me home and I'll screw your brains out," she promised looking deep into me with those hazel eyes. "I live only two blocks away on Park Avenue."

"Screw my brains out? I don't have a lot of brains to spare," I joked. "But let's give it a whirl."

Once we got to her apartment building, she started kissing me while we were still in the elevator. She started pulling up her dress and I saw that she was wearing a barely there thong. I gently stopped her from taking off her thong and pointed up to the camera.

"Let's not give your doorman a show... kissing okay, the skirt up is not okay," I insisted as I pulled down her dress.

Once in her apartment, we went at it like animals in heat, kissing and feeling each other up. When we broke for air from all of the kissing, I saw that Candy had this nauseous look on her face and she ran to her bathroom losing one of her high heels in the process. I tried to be a gentlemen and held her hair back while she threw up. With only one heel on and her skirt up in the air, her entire ass was revealed and it was one fine piece of ass.

When she stopped throwing up, she asked me to give her a few minutes to clean herself up. After several minutes in the bathroom, she came out totally nude. I could now see that she was entirely shaved. There was not even a small airstrip.

She threw her thong playfully at my face and then walked toward me, kissed me again, but then suddenly had that nauseous look again. Before I knew it, she was running back to the bathroom again. After another few minutes, I went into the bathroom, bringing tissues for her to clean her mouth and blow her nose. I led her to the bed and then, to her surprise, tucked her snugly in the bed.

"Are you angry at me?" she asked with a little tear in her eye.

"Not at all. I've been drunk and puked my brains out and so have most other people on the planet. Get a good night's sleep and let's try this again tomorrow night."

Candy gave me a sleepy smile as I kissed her on the cheek before heading out the door. I gave the doorman 50 dollars to check in on her later and left my business card with him. The next day I tried to call Candy, but she didn't pick up so I sent her a text message asking how she was. I got no response from her.

A couple of days later, I was at one of my car dealerships when a messenger arrived with a personal delivery for me. A note attached said that it was Candy who had sent it. Inside I saw several dress shirts from the haberdashery where I had met her. She had bought every single dress shirt that I had looked at while at the store where we'd met. Somehow, she had gotten each one of them mono-grammed with my initials.

I read the enclosed handwritten note:

Dearest Frank,

I have a confession to make to you. I am married. My husband and I had a big fight last month when I found out that he had sex with someone while on a business trip. We have been apart for a month and I was horny as hell. I was so touched by your thoughtfulness in getting me the chocolate bars, I just wanted to be single again for a day and maybe also wanted to get back at him by cheating also.

My husband called me today and I am going to give our marriage another try. You were such a gentlemen and so great to me the other night. Please accept these shirts as a token of how grateful I am for you just for

being you. I am sorry for not telling you the truth earlier.
I hope you can understand.

    Candy

Postscript: I never did see or talk to Candy again. Later, I heard she had moved with the hubby to the south of France. I decided to give away all the shirts that she had bought for me to friends. The shirts were so expensive, no one seemed to mind that they had the initials "FB" on them. All I can say is "Che Che La Femme" and all that stuff.

Secrets and Lies

(NINE)

When you think about it, how well do you really know anyone? When you meet a guy, does he say to you "Hi, I'm Bob, and I will cheat on you after two months of dating you" or "Hi, I'm Steve, I am really married but I won't tell you that until after I have slept with you"? It takes time to get to know someone, but even when you know someone for years, do you really know that person?

I was raised as a Christian but I suppose that at a certain point people decide about religion for themselves, whether it's to accept or renounce the one they were born into, or to join another. I guess that the turning point happened for me when I was twelve-years old. On that fateful day, my friend Barbara's mom, had come to the mall to pick up Barb and me along with our friend Gwen, and my seven-year-old cousin, Hosea, who was with me because I was looking after him. He was like a little brother to me.

As we were all sitting in the car on the drive home, Hosea kept insisting, "Buy me an ice cream, Nine."

"We're going to get something to eat for dinner first and then we can get an ice cream after," I answered.

Just as Barbara's mom made a left onto the highway a truck came barreling out of nowhere. The truck hit us from the right in the rear of the car. We went spinning at first and then for what seemed like an eternity, the car overturned multiple times before coming to a stop. We were all shaken up pretty badly. I had whiplash and had to wear a neck brace for a week. Barbara had broken her right arm, her mom had a broken ankle, and Gwen had a concussion.

But by all laws of physics, we should have been dead. The car was totaled. But the most amazing thing was that Hosea didn't have a scratch on him. As the car had spun around, he kept saying, "Nine, it is okay, it is okay. God is with us. God is with us." Did Hosea really see or feel the presence of God? How did he know that we would be safe?

Later, we learned that the truck driver had a fatal heart attack, which had caused him to lose control of the vehicle. And it wasn't until after we were all checked out of the emergency room that I was I finally able to ask Hosea why he was so calm and reassuring during and after the accident.

"I saw Jesus," he said.

"What do you mean, you saw him?" I asked.

"He was in the car with us when we got hit by the truck. He put his arms around me as the car turned over and over. He hugged me and that is why I didn't get hurt."

I just looked at him. For a few seconds I thought he was pulling my leg, but then I realized he was being honest. He was right. He didn't have a single bruise or mark on him and he wasn't afraid at all.

"Well what did he look like?" I asked.

"He was dressed as a king," he said smiling. "He seemed nice. He told me the hospital would give me ice cream."

Was he lying? Then I wondered, how did he know, at seven-years old, that the hospital would give him ice cream? From that day forward, I also was forever changed. I did really believe that God had protected all of us from dying that day. I still have a very small scar on my nose from that accident, which reminds me every day that I was saved. Over the years, Hosea never changed his story of what happened that day. Years later, he became a youth minister at the young age of twenty-one years old.

Hosea's brother Trent, was five years older than me. When I moved to New York, it was Trent who greeted me at the airport. Trent went to another church, not The Journey, since he liked more traditional music instead of the rock music of The Journey Church. Trent always seemed like a good Christian. He went to church each week and could quote The Bible. He and I would volunteer at a soup kitchen once a month to feed the homeless. He gave me an extra set of keys to his apartment, saying, "These are for you—just in case." As he said that, I thought to myself, just in case of what?

He was a hedge fund guy making more than a million dollars a year. He was a good-looking guy and had no problem getting dates, but never seemed to have a long-term girlfriend.

One day I got a call from his office. Trent hadn't gone to work for three days and I was listed as his emergency contact person. I told them I would go to his place and see what the situation was. The moment I entered his apartment, I smelled an awful smell. Immediately, I thought, it couldn't be, he is only in his early thirties.

But when I went into the bedroom, I screamed at the sight of his already decomposing naked body. That image of him is something I can't get out of my head. I ran out of the apartment and called 911. The autopsy revealed that it was a heart attack caused by a total blockage of one of his main arteries. Trent was super fit and actually was into bodybuilding, but since he worked out so much, he didn't really think to watch his diet and still ate lots of saturated fats like red meat and bacon. He hated doctors and never went for annual check-ups.

The family shipped Trent's body back home to the Midwest for the funeral. Montoya was the only one of my close friends in New York who knew Trent. However, Montoya was in London visiting his parents, so I didn't want to trouble him. Besides, I would have the support of many family members at the funeral.

After the funeral, my cousin Hosea flew back to New York with me and for the rest of the weekend, he went through Trent's apartment to collect all the items of sentimental value and then gave the rest away to the Salvation Army. Hosea had given me Trent's office computer and asked me to return it to Trent's office the following week. When I took Hosea to the airport, as we were saying our goodbyes, he mentioned that Trent's office had called him about the computer and they'd asked that anything personal be removed from it before returning it. It sounded simple enough.

Later that day, when I went into his computer, I saw numerous downloaded items on the desktop. I clicked on the first item and was horrified to see a video of Trent naked and having sex with a woman. I clicked it off immediately and went to the next download. It was another video of Trent having sex, but with a different woman. I kept clicking through the files on his desktop, which all turned out to be videos of Trent with various women.

By the end of it all, I felt numb. He had more than forty videos of himself having sex with different women. It appeared as if these women didn't know they were being videotaped. He had always been into electronic gadgets and would create silly little videos with his smart phone all the time. In fact, instead of sending greeting cards or e-cards, he often made an annual video greeting for his friends and family.

I felt sick to my stomach thinking about his videos. I remember he had a curtain near his bed. I think that is where he hid the camera, judging from the angle in which the videos of him having sex were shot. But why? How could he do this? I thought he was a good guy. How could he do this without these women's permission? How could he do this even with their permission? I had known him my entire life. Everyone thought he was as good a person, as sincere a Christian as his brother, Hosea.

Then I realized that I was Trent's "shovel buddy," the person you entrust to clean up your secret crap after you've died. But I felt like this responsibility had been forced upon me. Trent had enlisted me to be his shovel buddy without asking for my permission, just as he hadn't asked the permission of the women who he had secretly taped.

My sadness regarding Trent's untimely death had turned into anger and resentment. How could he put me in this position? How could God put me in this position? Should I tell his parents? Should I tell his brother, Hosea, who looked up to his older brother? Would it destroy everyone else's faith? My faith was shaken. He made me wonder, how many other people carry around these secrets and lies that they don't tell anyone else?

Feeling completely depressed and wanting to withdraw from the world, I took another bereavement day off from work. Finally, I caved in; I had to talk to someone, so I called Hosea on Skype. I told him everything. He didn't seem to be surprised.

"I am not completely surprised to hear this because Trent had been struggling with sex addiction. I am sorry that you had to find out about it this way. Nothing turned up when I went through Trent's apartment, so I thought it would be best if I not mention anything to you about it."

"What?! I can't believe this! You knew?"

"For about two years now, he had been going on and off to a twelve step program. It seemed to be helping. I really encouraged him and he agreed to put a software program on his computer that allowed me to see whatever websites he visited. It was a way to stop him from downloading porn from the web. But I am sorry to find out, that he started making his own movies to watch on his work computer."

"This is terrible. How many other people know?"

"Just you and me. Trent was weak when it came to sex. He couldn't control himself and he needed help. I tried to help him. I never thought he would die at such a young age. I thought that he would have more time to work through this. He is in God's hands now."

"God? How could God let this happen? You're a minister. Tell me. How?"

"This isn't God's fault. He gives us free will. Trent is responsible for his own deeds and actions. People are weak and that is why they need a higher power than themselves. Remember the car accident we were in? I think of that almost every day. I realize that God knows everything about me and you, as well as Trent and yet he still loves us. That is why I am a youth minister, so I can help others feel God's love."

After talking with Hosea, I felt less angry at Trent, but the images of his dead body and the images of him having sex with so many women were burned into my brain. I felt like Trent's death was a blow to my faith. I kept thinking about the other people in my life. How well do I know my parents? How well do I know Montoya? How well do I know anyone?

There is always that person they interview on the news who lived right next to the serial killer and the neighbor always says the same thing: "He (or she) was quiet, kept to himself/herself, and seemed nice." It's scary, you never really know about people.

Rode Hard and Hung Wet
(MONTOYA and Frank)

You would think that you never bump into anyone in New York City. I mean with more than eight million people, what is the likelihood of you bumping into people who you know? But the reality is that single people tend to congregate in the same watering holes, so to speak. It's no different than gazelles on the Serengeti. Whether at French Tuesdays, some new club in the Meatpacking District, a trendy rooftop bar, or some museum gala, people congregate in the same places, like a herd of water buffalo.

So, it is really no surprise to see the same people over and over again if you are a frequent attender of networking events, parties, and mixers in Manhattan. In fact, you could say that New York City is the world's biggest small town. If you network enough, it seems like everyone is a friend of a friend or someone's ex.

I had met Bonita at the opening of a member's-only preview at the Metropolitan Museum of Art. She was from Columbia, thirty-years old, very sexy and was in public relations. We hit it off immediately. She liked my British accent and my sense of humor. She would pronounce my name as Mon-toy-a. We went out for a month and the sex was great. Bonita's older sister Maria from San Francisco was visiting for the weekend. Maria was as pretty as Bonita, but older. She looked about forty-five-years old and acted very much like an older protective sister to Bonita. Everything was great until I took them both with me to my friend Vanessa's party.

When we arrived at the party, I immediately introduced Bonita and Maria to Vanessa and I promptly got each of the ladies a glass of white wine. Vanessa had an assortment of snacks for her guests. As the ladies sipped their wine, they nibbled on some cheese, and I started eating some sushi rolls. Tara was also there so I introduced the ladies to her. Just as I was wondering where Frank was, I saw him standing in the corner of the room with a look on his face that I had never seen before. He looked furious. I excused myself to Bonita and Maria and walked over to him.

"Frank, you seem upset," I said.

"How do you know that woman?" he demanded.

"Which woman? The younger one is my new girlfriend, Bonita, and the older one is her sister, Maria who is visiting from out of town."

"From San Francisco?" he asked still with a tone of anger.

"Yes, how did you know?"

"The older one is my former girlfriend. The one who screwed me over!" he said a little too loudly.

Frank had told me about his ex, but he never mentioned her name. About five years ago, before I had met him, he had fallen head over heels for a Columbian woman, who I now realized was Maria. He had met her when he attended a charity gala and they ended up dating for an entire year. Frank wanted to marry her and he proposed and she said yes. But then, she decided to move to San Francisco and wanted Frank to move there also. He was in love with her so he decided to sell his condo and was preparing to move his business over there.

However, only two weeks after he arrived in San Francisco, she told him that she had major doubts about the relationship and had fallen out of love with him. He demanded to know why she didn't tell him this before he had moved to California, sold his condo, and made plans to move his business. She kept saying that she couldn't offer an explanation. But he kept pressing her for an explanation until she gave in.

Maria told him that when she first met him, she was so attracted to him that she went to a voodoo doctor, who she paid to cast a love spell on him. She said the spell worked a little too well and that he had fallen too much in love with her and now he had become boring to her. He didn't know how to respond at first and just stood there silently in shock.

So, he asked for the engagement ring back. When she refused to give it back to him, he yelled, "The hell with you!" Then, he left and never looked back. He tore up her photos, threw out anything that reminded him of her, and practically vowed never to fall in love again. After that, he wasn't serious about any woman. He dated constantly, he shagged like it was going out of season, but he never established a long-term relationship for the entire five years after this woman broke his heart.

"She looks like she was rode hard and hung wet," Frank said still angry.

"What does that mean?"

"It's an American expression. It means she is a whore who has not aged well. She is only thirty-five years old," Frank said.

"Bugger! She looks at least ten-years older," I added.

"Look, Montoya, I am going to leave the party now. If I stay, I am likely to start making a fool of myself by cursing this skank bitch out in public."

"I totally understand. Look, Frank, I like Bonita but obviously I didn't know who her sister was. But now that I know this, I can't, I just can't get serious about Bonita."

"I'm not telling you what to do in your relationships."

"You don't have to Frank. I have never seen you this angry. You and I are close friends. How could I possibly get serious with Bonita now?"

Frank left the party. As he was leaving, Maria and he caught each other's eyes. Frank looked like he wanted to kill her, but he immediately turned away and exited the party without saying a word to her. I walked back to Bonita and Maria.

"Do you know the man who just left?" Maria asked.

"Yes, he is a good friend of mine."

"We used to date. He looks like he has aged well," she said.

Later that night, I shared a cab home with Bonita and Maria. After I dropped them off, I couldn't stop thinking about what had happened between Frank and Maria. Maria and Bonita were very close. I now knew that if I got involved with Bonita, that her sister would also be a part of my life. But knowing what I did about what had happened between Maria and Frank, I decided that I'd have to end it with Bonita.

Cane and Not Able

(FRANK, Montoya, Luana and Tara)

I left Vanessa's party in a hurry because I had seen my bitch ex-girlfriend Maria. She looked aged and worn like the whore she is. Montoya was just being a ladies' man, as usual. He had no clue what a ball buster his new girlfriend's sister was. All my memories of the breakup were going through my head. And wouldn't you know it, just my luck, it was pouring outside. I tried to hail a cab for fifteen minutes and finally gave up. That's the problem with living in Manhattan, whenever it rains; everyone seems to be trying to hail a cab at the same time.

I took out my phone to call up Uber but my phone had died so I decided to take the subway home. I sat down in one of the two-seaters near the door separating the subway cars. As I was waiting for the train to leave the station, I saw that a black woman, probably in her early fifties, had walked out of the next car and was trying to open the door right by my seat. But the door seemed to be locked. I saw her turn around and try to go back into the other car, but that door was now stuck. Realizing that she was now trapped between the two cars, the woman started to panic as the subway train started moving. She looked like she was afraid to fall between the cars. So, I got up and tried to pry the door open to let her in. The subway train was now zooming at fifty miles per hour.

She started pounding on the door and started screaming hysterically for help. I kept trying to leverage all my weight and to put my hip into it to push the door open. Meanwhile, I saw that people on other side of her, in the other car were also trying to open the door for her. Finally, after what seemed like an eternity but was actually less than a minute, the people on the other side got the door to open and she got safely back into the other car. The door on my side was still locked. Unfortunately, I hadn't been able to push the door open or to unlock it.

I went home and didn't think anything more of it until the next morning, when I woke up with numbness in my right leg and hip. As I tried to move my right leg, it felt like I had dislocated it. When I stood up, my leg buckled and I fell down. I picked myself up using the wall as leverage and hopped over to my cell phone. I called 911 since I was unable to walk. An ambulance came and took me to the hospital where they X-rayed my leg and took an MRI. They told me I had torn some ligaments attached to my hipbone, needed to walk with a cane for three months, and to undergo daily physical therapy. I thought great, this is what you get for trying to be the hero and save a woman from her death. But the real surprise was the orthopedic doctor telling me I couldn't have sex for three months. I looked at him as if he were speaking in a foreign language.

"Three months without sex!" I yelled out loud, not realizing how loud I was until I heard myself. "Three months!"

"Sorry, Mr. Branigan, but your hip has to heal," the doctor stated firmly.

It seemed like God, fate, the universe, or whatever you want to call it, was just adding insult to injury after me seeing my ex the night before. She pops up back in my life and, once again, my life is a disaster. There is a fine line between love and hatred. Once I had loved her, but now I felt intense hatred toward her.

The next time I saw Tara and Montoya, I walked in using a cane and they said that the cane made me look even more distinguished and dapper. I know they were trying to make me feel better, but the cane just made me feel pretty damn old. How do you pick up a twenty-five-year-old woman with a cane in one hand?

I went to my first physical therapy session at a midtown health club. I did ten minutes on the exercise bike, and then knee lifts and squats using elastic bands. After that, I had a heat pad placed on my hip for twenty minutes. My physical therapist's name was Leah Patel, and thank God she was pretty. She was Indian and looked like she was in her mid-thirties. But it was her personality that really stood out. The part of the session I looked forward to most was when Leah stood on the table I was lying down on and placed my foot on her shoulder. She then used all her weight to stretch out my hip and leg. What was great about it was that she talked to me the entire time. She was a very talkative, bubbly, and positive person. Though I felt like an invalid, she was a daily cup of good cheer.

As I went through physical therapy, I couldn't stop thinking about how my bitch of an ex-girlfriend had screwed me one more time. I couldn't have sex. I was in pain, and I felt like a grandfather having to walk around with a damn cane all the time. Instead of just drinking wine, I started drinking Jack and Cokes. I found myself losing count of how many drinks I'd had. Some of my friends noticed this and told me to take it easy, but I needed something to help me through this crisis. They say hindsight is 20/20 vision, but when you are going through something, you aren't always thinking clearly.

Things came to a head at a party Montoya held in his apartment. He had about fifty people in his two-bedroom apartment. Montoya had so many beautiful women at his party and just my luck; I was there with a cane in one hand. I lost track of how many Jack and Cokes that I drank. At the end of the night, seeing the state that I was in, Montoya asked me if I wanted to just stay the night and Tara offered to take me home. But I refused. I was no invalid. I could take care of myself. Montoya's friend Luana was at the same party, so I walked up to her and said, "Hey, are you still interested in having me screw you two times a week?"

"Look, that was a while ago and I was different then," she answered politely.

"You think you are too good for me? Because of the cane? You bitch! You damned whore! I bet all of New York City has screwed you!" I yelled out.

Montoya came over and told me to calm down.

"Back the hell off!" I yelled at him.

Tara came over and pleaded with me, "Frank, please. You aren't yourself. Please let me take you home."

"Do I look like I need a caretaker? I am not an old man that you have to take care of, even though I have a cane!"

That was the last thing I remember. I guess I passed out. Montoya had let me sleep it off in his apartment and given me several cups of coffee. I don't remember the coffee, but the next morning I reeked of coffee and Jack. Montoya had made me toast and tea for breakfast. I took some of the toast and immediately threw up all over Montoya's living room floor. Tara had also stayed over in Montoya's apartment to watch over me. She helped Montoya to clean the floor.

"I know it has been hard on you, Frank, to see your ex and then to immediately have this hip problem. But you can't keep drinking like this," Tara said trying to comfort me.

"Tara, I am very sorry for yelling at you. Montoya, I'm also very sorry for yelling at you. You two are really great friends. Better than I deserve," I responded surprised that a tear came rolling out of my left eye and down my cheek. I wiped the tear away embarrassed.

"Frank, there's no need for apologies. I have been pissed drunk myself and done some pretty embarrassing things," Montoya said.

"No, it was totally uncalled for. I have been having this pity party for myself long enough and this was really hitting rock bottom. How many people did I embarrass myself in front of?" I asked.

"The person who was embarrassed last night wasn't you, it was Luana. What you said to her was really bad. I think, not only do you owe her a huge apology, but you'd better find some way to make amends with her," Tara said.

"I agree. You need to make it up to her," Montoya added.

"I know. All the things I held in that I wanted to say to Maria came out against the wrong person. Luana was just an innocent bystander," I admitted.

I went cold turkey from that day and stopped drinking. I wasn't going to let my ex destroy my life twice in a row. Tara and Montoya arranged for me to meet with Luana after they saw that I had stopped the drinking binge.

Luana was gracious and accepted my apology. I said that I wanted to do something for her to make up for what I said. She surprised me when she said that she needed a babysitter. She belonged to an all-women's group that got together once a week for brunch and sometimes for an entire day on the weekends. Many of the women were married with children. For one month, the babysitter who watched over all the kids would be going home for her annual visit to her family in Croatia. So, Luana suggested that I babysit the assortment of rugrats for that one month. Me babysitting? I reluctantly agreed. Since I still had about a month left using my cane and felt like I was now in the dating minor leagues, I figured that it wouldn't be that big of a sacrifice.

The arrangement was for all of the parents to drop off their kids at Luana's, before I arrived. Luana usually came home first to relieve me of my babysitting duties before the parents came to pick up their kids. The kids were actually quite well behaved. There was a black kid named Ernest, an Indian girl named Shanti, a white kid named Barry, and a black girl named Sheryl. So, I didn't really feel like I was babysitting. It was really more like supervising a play date for the kids. I was simply overseeing all of these kids and keeping them out of harm's way.

Every day at lunchtime, I went to see my physical therapist. I started to realize that this was the longest "relationship" I have had since my ex-girlfriend five years ago. I began to look forward to having witty conversations with Leah and absorbing her positive attitude. When I finally got rid of the cane, you'd think I'd want to end this dry spell, but I didn't want to risk throwing out my hip again. So, I continued to abstain from having sex and drinking.

One afternoon Luana came back home early from her women's group meeting and with her was none other than Leah. I couldn't believe it. In the small, small world of New York City, I had been babysitting her six-year old daughter Shanti, without knowing that Leah was Shanti's mother.

During physical therapy, Leah was dressed in jeans and a T-shirt. But she was now wearing a short, sexy skirt, and her hair, which was usually pulled back into a ponytail, was loosely flowing down past her shoulders. I never noticed her cleavage during my sessions with her, but now she had three buttons of her blouse open. She looked hot! Luana could see that Leah and I recognized each other and said. "Why am I not surprised that you know each other? Frank, you seem to know all the pretty women."

The last week of my physical therapy also happened to be my last week of babysitting duties for Luana. The next time I saw Leah for my physical therapy session, she arrived in a T-shirt and jeans. I pictured her the last time I saw her, and started mentally undressing her. When she held up my leg to her shoulder to stretch my leg, I got a hard on and tried to position myself to hide it, but it was clear as day to Leah. She looked at me and said teasing, "I'm happy to see you too."

I asked her if both she and Shanti would like to go for a picnic on Sunday in Central Park, but I was actually asking her out on a date. It was the first time I'd been on a date that involved a six-year old. Leah could see the rapport that Shanti and I had developed as we talked about her class pet Thomas, the turtle, and when Shanti called me "Uncle Frank."

After the picnic, Leah invited me back to her place and we ordered in and watched a Pixar film with Shanti. When Shanti went to sleep, I took my first glass of wine since the drunken binge. I stopped at one drink, gave Leah one kiss on the lips goodnight, and said I would call her.

Leaving her apartment, I realized how meeting Leah and her daughter was the direct result of me trying to be a hero. And then I thought, in every movie the hero always gets the girl. Maybe I should have tried to save someone's life a long, long time ago?

What's Below the Surface?

(TARA)

Frank's drunken outburst in Montoya's apartment made me think of a previous relationship that I'd had with a man who had serious anger issues. Frank's anger had been triggered by the painful memories of his ex, and he realized that he had too much to drink and immediately went cold turkey. He was nothing like Mattias who was in denial and clueless as to the root of his anger. Sometimes, you just don't know what is below the surface of that iceberg, until your version of the Titanic hits it.

The memories came flooding back into my head.

Mattias had his favorite band, Megadeth, blaring in the car on the drive home, which was not unusual, but he had been uncharacteristically quiet.

So, I broke the ice and said at the top of my lungs, "It was fun to get to know some of your co-workers better at the office party tonight."

"Yeah, I noticed you talking to Tom most of the night."

I had met Tom once before through Mattias. Tom was a massive guy at 6 foot 7. He definitely had an imposing presence. He towered over everyone, including Mattias who was 6 foot 2. Of the two, I definitely thought that Mattias was more attractive. He had a very well-sculpted physique from years of weight training. Tom and Mattias were about same age and had started at the company at around the same time. The two of them also had a lot in common, so they became fast friends outside of the office.

Both were outdoorsy types. They often went on weekend camping trips and in the past they had taken vacations "with the boys" that sounded like crazy college spring break vacations. That was in their younger, single days, before Mattias and I had met. Mattias had always spoken so fondly of Tom and their friendship. He really kind of looked up to Tom and thought of him as a brother. Mattias was an only child. Tom was not married yet, and seemed to enjoy being a bachelor and the freedom he had. It suited him since he was so spontaneous and carefree.

Mattias said that Tom would always tell him what a lucky man he was for snagging me. And that being single was not always what it was cracked up to be. But I think that secretly Mattias must have thought the grass was greener on the other side, as he saw the many beautiful women who seemed to walk in and out of the revolving doors of Tom's life. Mattias and I had been married for about a year when I'd finally met Tom again at the office party that night.

"Well, Tom is one of your best friends; he seems like a brother to you. And I don't know him all that well, so I thought I'd take a chance to know him a bit better," I answered.

As the music continued to blare and just as the percussion kicked in, Mattias turned up the volume.

"Yeah, you looked really hot tonight. You were flirting with him!" he yelled.

"You were jealous? Don't be silly."

Mattias jacked up the volume and rolled down the window. He started singing the lyrics at the top of his lungs. He was speeding now.

"Mattias, could you turn down the volume? I can't talk to you like this."

His hands gripped the steering wheel and he looked straight ahead as if in a trance and continued singing at the top of his lungs. He had always liked to play Megadeth. That was nothing new, but the way he was driving, blaring the music and ignoring me, it scared me. I knew that there was no talking to him when he got like this. I just braced myself as he sped down the freeway and sharply exited the ramp.

When he parked the car in the driveway and turned off the ignition, and it was finally silent for a moment I said, "What was that all about?! Was that really necessary? I felt like a hostage in the car."

"You felt like a hostage?! Well, then, don't let me keep you all locked up! I saw the way you were looking at Tom."

Mattias turned to me with an angry look on his face and smacked me in the stomach knocking the wind out of me. He got out of the car and slammed the door shut, leaving me there sitting alone in the driveway. I sat there in shock and sobbed. I had always known that Mattias had a temper, but he had never laid a hand on me. He'd always been very competitive with Tom and somehow it had finally gotten the best of him that night.

It was the beginning of a downward spiral for our relationship. When we first started dating, I had told Mattias that I thought he was not ambitious enough. He had interpreted that to mean that he somehow did not measure up in my eyes, and that he was not enough. I think that somehow, he never seemed to recover from that blow to his ego. Perhaps some of his insecurities had finally gotten the best of him and led him to pick a fight with me.

He apologized over and over and I tried to forgive him, but I could not forget or trust that he'd be able to control his temper. I wanted him to seek help to work through his anger management issues. He didn't. We went back and forth on the issue for a few months. It was a helpless, frustrating feeling. After he hit me, I looked back on things and realized that there had been a pattern.

Once when we were still dating, we were playing a game of *Frogger* and when I had won three games in a row against him, he got so furious that he punched a hole in the side of the arcade machine. On another occasion, we were at a deli ordering sandwiches. Mattias had ordered a Coke, but when he opened the bottle and took a sip of it, he realized that it was a root beer. He spit it out and smashed the bottle on the floor, yelling, "What the hell is this?! I hate root beer. I ordered a Coke!" I recall that he had made a few other scenes like this, too.

All along, I had chalked up these incidents to his headstrong, competitive nature. He was a very physical guy. He was really into contact sports like football, rugby, and martial arts. In college he'd been on the wrestling team. He loved sparring, and he brought that physicality into the bedroom. In fact, there was something about his animalistic aggressiveness that turned me on. I liked his tough manliness, but at the same time, he was very sensitive and passionate. But what I thought was just a passionate, fiery temper turned out to be anger management issues that needed to be worked out.

It wasn't until much later, after we had finally divorced that I understood the whole picture. Mattias' father, Alfred, had always treated me like a daughter; he had been ill for some time before then. Even after the divorce, we remained close and I would frequently visit him in the hospital. When Alfred passed away, I went to the funeral.

Mattias was there with Tom, who was comforting him. When I saw them, in a flash I knew. Then Mattias confirmed it.. He told me that he was bisexual, but that he had decided that he preferred men, and that he was with Tom now. It all made sense—the camping trips together and his admiration for Tom. Mattias had been jealous about Tom, not me. He was jealous of Tom paying attention to me, but he didn't know it at the time. He hadn't fully recognized his feelings for Tom. Perhaps, that's what Mattias needed, someone who was more an equal, someone who could match and handle his aggression.

Most of my friends in New York don't know that I've been married before. Frank was the only one who knew since he has known me since I was a teenager. I have no hard feelings or regrets about what happened with Mattias. I walked out of that situation and realized that I am a lot stronger than I thought I was.

When I went through the divorce, I found out who my real friends were—they were the ones who stood by me and were really there for me. What I learned about relationships is that sometimes the things that don't work far outweigh what does work. Realizing what isn't working is half the battle. Then, you can decide what to do about it and whether it's salvageable or not. It'll save you a lot of heartache in the future.

Understanding what Mattias went through has helped me be more sympathetic to women and men who struggle with their sexuality. Finding love is hard enough, but when you add denial of your sexual preferences, it obviously causes many complications. Straight, gay, or bi? If you have to ask this question of yourself, I think you shouldn't be afraid of embracing the answer.

YEAR II

WINTER

Meet Me at the Corner

(MONTOYA, Tara and Frank)

I had met Svetlana at an art gallery exhibit opening in Williamsburg. She immediately liked my British accent and I could tell she was definitely attracted to me. She was beautiful and voluptuous, with red hair and green eyes and wore what appeared to be a push-up bra, although she didn't need it since she was at least a C cup. The push-up bra made it appear as if she had a D cup.

She didn't have an email address and said she wanted people to only call her. She also wouldn't accept any text messages. That should have told me something, but when you see a beautiful woman, your little brain is doing most of the thinking. She told me she was from some Slavic country with a "stan" at the end of it. Was it Kurdistan? Or Kazakhstan? Her accent made it difficult to figure out which "stan" country it was and I wasn't trying to press the issue with her. She explained that her first language was one of those "stan" languages, then Russian, with English being a distant third.

We exchanged numbers and I suggested right there at the art opening that we should get together for dinner sometime soon. I told her that I wanted to take her to Amber, a nice Pan-Asian restaurant, known for its big Buddha statue. Since it was early December and it would be cold outside, I told her that I would meet her inside at the bar.

She said, "No, meet me at the corner."

I asked, "Why the corner?"

She replied, "Because."

"No, it will be cold outside."

"I need you to meet me on the corner."

"You can call me on my mobile when you arrive," I repeated. "I will be sitting at the bar."

"No! I need you to meet me at the corner."

So, then I thought, maybe she is a spy. Maybe she does hand-offs of secret documents on corners and she has mistaken me for someone from MI6. Finally, I gave in and said okay. Yes, I would meet her at the corner.

When the day arrived, I ended up standing in the freezing cold on a street corner waiting for her. Finally, my mobile phone rang.

"Where are you?" asked Svetlana.

"I am standing right in front of the Amber restaurant."

"Where are you?" she asked again.

"I am at the corner of 70th and Columbus, just like I said I'd be."

"I am at the corner of 70th and Columbus, but I don't see you," she said with a hint of frustration in her voice.

"How can that be? Whichever corner you are on, you need to cross the street to the correct corner."

"Which corner?"

Trying to hide my exasperation, I said to her, "The one with the big sign saying Amber."

"I don't see it. Can you come get me?"

I thought to myself, maybe something happened, like she lost her contacts and was blind as a bat. So, I gave in again and searched the other three corners to find her. Blimey, you have to laugh sometimes at the ridiculousness of some dating situations. I eventually found her and walked her over to Amber. Once inside the restaurant, we were promptly seated in the back section near the Buddha statue. After the waiter handed us the menus and Svetlana took a quick look at it, she put the menu down and promptly asked me to order her some fish.

"Fish?" I asked, hoping that this would prompt her to be more specific. "You do realize that sushi is the specialty here and that they have many varieties when it comes to fish."

She didn't laugh. She had a deadpan look on her face.

"Order me some fish! You decide for me," she said in a somewhat annoyed and bossy tone.

I picked the dragon roll sushi and pointed it out to her on the menu. From the way she looked at it, it suddenly dawned on me what the problem was.

"You can't read? Can you?" I asked incredulously. It all made sense. That's why she didn't use email, or accept text messages. That's why she insisted on meeting at the corner and why I had to cross the street to get her to the correct corner, because she couldn't read the sign with the word Amber.

"No! That is not true!" she angrily replied. "I can read my language and also Russian. But just not English."

"How long have you lived in the States?"

"Ten years."

"Bollocks! How can you live in the States for ten years and not know how to read English? If I lived in Moscow for ten years, don't you think I would have taken at least one Russian language class?"

She explained that she sold cosmetics to the Russian emigrants of Brighton Beach, and that her mobile phone and email and text messages were all written in Russian. She said that most of the men she's met just wanted her for her body and that she thought I wasn't like most men.

"But still, you never thought of taking a class in English?"

She just looked at me blankly. I ordered her the dragon sushi roll, and we ended the date with us making out in the back of a taxicab.

But later, I thought to myself, what would happen when it got even colder outside? Would she expect me to freeze my arse off always waiting for her on some corner in New York City? She was quite beautiful and I wondered if I could put up with always standing out in the freezing cold waiting for her. But Svetlana wasn't going to wait for me to decide.

Two days later, I was having a drink with Tara and Frank at Mr. Dennehy's in the West Village. It is a good bar for watching football games (and I'm not referring to American football). I was watching my favorite team, Arsenal, play when I got a call from Svetlana asking why I hadn't called her. I said that I was sorry for not responding sooner and that I was planning on calling her, but that I had been busy at work on a priority project. I mentally pictured her and instantly invited her to join us at the restaurant. I told her the address of where we were.

"This place should be easy for you to find since it is the only corner of the four corners where Con Ed is doing street work outside of the restaurant."

I told Frank and Tara what to expect—a beautiful woman with a hot body who can't read English. Svetlana came in wearing a long coat, walked right over to me, and put her arms around me in a tight embrace, not letting go as she gave me a long, passionate kiss, while sticking her tongue in my mouth. I tried to introduce her to both Frank and Tara but Svetlana seemed totally oblivious to their presence and only focused on me.

When Frank held out his hand to shake hers, she totally ignored him. Frank muttered, "What the hell" under his breath and Tara looked on at the scene with disbelief. Svetlana appeared to be high or on something, so I suggested she relax and sit down. She proceeded to take off her coat revealing a tight sweater, still never looking at or acknowledging Frank or Tara. Next, she started peeling her sweater off, revealing a sheer blouse with an even more see-through bra underneath. As she sat on my lap you could see that her skirt was so short that it barely covered her private parts. I looked over at my two friends who were now looking at an essentially topless woman sitting in my lap across from them. And by the way, I was right. She was a C cup.

Meanwhile, the male patrons in the bar were nudging each other and pointing in my direction. I tried to get her to put the sweater back on but she didn't want to. Instead, she started whispering in my ear, saying that she wanted me to take her home to her apartment and teach her English. It was clear to me that she wanted me to do a lot more than teach her English. The woman wanted to be shagged on the spot. If I suggested going to the loo and shagging her there, she would have said yes. When I told her that I couldn't just leave my two friends, but that afterwards I could go somewhere else with her, she put her hand on my leg.

"I really want you to come home with me," she insisted in a voice that was sweet yet demanding.

"Sorry, I really can't go right now."

She immediately got up, put on her sweater and said, "Well, goodbye then!" and exited the bar.

Once she had left, Frank and Tara both cracked up.

"What the hell was that?" Tara asked. "She was obviously high on something."

"Why didn't you go with her? She wanted to screw your brains out," Frank added.

"We only had one date and we made out for a long time, but there was no shagging. I guess she was impatient. However, I am positive she will find some guy to shag her tonight. It is a shame though; I was going to shag her when we had our second date. But now I am concerned that she is a drug user, which is a big no-no in my book."

"Illiterate and high, boy do you know how to pick 'em," Frank joked.

Men Who Love Blow Jobs and the Women Who Love Them

(FRANK)

Like most men, I have always loved it when women give me blow jobs. After all, that is probably how a lot of guys are first introduced to sex. If you think back to your firsts—in high school or even college (for you late bloomers)—there was that initial feeling of excitement the first time you got close to touching a woman's tits, even when she was still clothed. But that was nothing compared to the first time you put your hand under her blouse and reached up under her bra to actually feel her nipples.

I also remember the first time I started stroking a woman's bare legs. Her name was Prudence and she was the hottest girl in my high school. We were making out in the back row of a movie theater. She was wearing a miniskirt and as I started stroking her legs, I realized that she wasn't wearing any pantyhose. I finally got the nerve to put my hand between her legs. I kept feeling around with one hand while stroking her inner thigh with the other. I made it way past her panties and as my fingers explored her, she became wetter and wetter.

I put her hand on my dick, which was hard by now and pressing against the inside of my jeans. She started to rub my dick. Then, I looked around to make sure no one was looking, as I unzipped my jeans. Prudence and I looked at each other in the dark and she knew exactly what I wanted. She leaned over and pulled out my dick, which she started licking up and down and finally put it in her mouth. Even though she had acted coy, she seemed to have done this before. She didn't stop until I was ready to explode. I felt like pounding my chest, like King Kong on top of the Empire State Building. There were a lot of firsts that day—it was my first time exploring between a woman's legs, my first blow job, and my first semi-public sexual experience.

So began my love of blow jobs. Every man probably has a story like this or remembers his first one. Blow jobs are always good and even better when they happen at the most unexpected times. I guess that's what made Speedy so hard to resist.

One of my exes, Dee Dee, was always one to push the envelope. I was in Las Vegas on a business trip with her, and I swear, there's something about Vegas and hotel rooms that just puts you "in the mood." Of course, we could not keep our hands off of each other and, things were getting hot and heavy in the room when my cell phone alarm went off reminding me that I had a video conference call scheduled.

As soon as I realized this, I quickly put my shirt back on and got onto the video conference call. Dee Dee, however, decided that she was not through with me yet. So, she got down in front of my chair and started giving me a blow job while I was in the middle of the video conference call. I don't think anyone caught on when I exclaimed "Yes!" upon hearing that we'd made a multi-million dollar deal. They had no idea what pleasure there was behind that "yes."

My favorite blow jobs have been while driving. I love driving long distances with miles and miles of open road ahead of me. And of course I like driving fast, especially driving through those S curves in the road. That takes some skill and it's such a thrill. Putting these two things together— the sensation of speeding along a highway while getting blown—it makes me feel like the king of the road. It might sound dangerous, but I'm always in total control and focused on the road while driving. If I know I'm going to be drinking I just won't drive at all, so I haven't gotten into any accidents or had any dangerous close calls. But I did have a different sort of "close call" once. I was driving upstate with this girl, Betty, who I was seeing at the time. For much of the drive, I had one hand on the steering wheel and the other up her skirt. After making her sopping wet, she moaned and screamed until she couldn't take it any longer and came.

I looked over at her as she rested. Then, she gave me a sidelong look, winked at me, and said, "Okay, now it's your turn." She leaned over to unzip my pants and return the favor. She put her mouth on my dick and rubbed it with her tongue as she started slowly going up and down. She was really good at giving blow jobs, maybe a little too good because before I knew it, I heard a siren. My heart started racing as I thought, oh great that's just what I need, to get pulled over by a cop. I looked in the rearview mirror and saw an ambulance, which was a relief. So I slowed down to yield to the ambulance and pulled over. Then, Betty "finished her job."

Now that I was with Leah, I couldn't wait for her to give me a blow job. She was fantastic—a real lady who was elegant and sexy at the same time. I took her to all the best restaurants in town but she also liked to cook for me at home so that I could also spend time with her daughter, Shanti. The three of us would have dinner together on Saturday each week at her place. After Shanti was all tucked in, it was "bedtime" for Leah and me. Nothing was off-limits in the bedroom, except we had to be quiet for Shanti's sake.

I would buy Leah the sleaziest of lingerie outfits for her to wear like crotch-less body stockings, see through teddies, risqué outfits from Agent Provocateur, you name it. In the bedroom she was as wild as she was elegant in public. Outside of the bedroom, she was discretely provocative in her phone calls, voicemails, and texts as she would repeatedly give double entendre messages filled with sexual innuendos and outright blatant dirty talk. She kept me in a heightened sense of anticipation every day. All day long I looked forward to leaving work and seeing whether she would fulfill the acts she promised in her messages. Every man's dream, a lady in the public and a wild woman in the bedroom.

The first time Leah and I had sex, I started by going down on her. Then, I kept giving her "the look." Women recognize this look. You know, when a man motions to his dick and tries to telepathically inform the woman to suck his dick. Well, Leah just wasn't getting my subtle hints. I tried to gently move her head to my dick. She pulled away and went to French kiss me instead. Finally I said, "Suck me." She ignored my request and moved on top of me and we had amazing sex. Finally, as I lay in bed afterward, I just had to get the issue out in the open.

"I really like it when a woman gives me a blow job," I informed her.

"Yes, I could tell from all the not-so-subtle hints," she responded. "But I don't really do blow jobs."

"What? I thought all women do blow jobs."

"Well maybe, I don't want to spoil you yet," Leah said playing coy.

The second and third time we had sex, I went through this ritual of saying, "Suck me," which she ignored each time. That's when I realized that we had a big problem. I didn't know why she wouldn't give me a blow job. She could tell that I was getting frustrated, so she reached into her nightstand, pulled out a mouthpiece and showed it to me.

"What is that?" I asked.

"I have TMJ and I usually wear this mouthpiece at night while sleeping, which prevents me from grinding my teeth. I didn't want to wear it the first few times we went to bed. But now I think you should know about it."

"So, that is why you don't want to give me a blow job?"

"It's not that I don't want to please you that way, but I need to be careful. When I was with my ex, I'd give him blow jobs but it caused me some pain and led to a major flare up. It was so serious that I actually had difficulty swallowing and eating."

"I see."

"I don't want to risk something like that happening again. And I didn't want to start things off by setting a certain precedent or giving you false expectations."

"I don't see why you didn't tell me this before."

"I'm sorry. I guess I'd been kind of avoiding the topic. I knew that I'd have to talk to you about this. I hope that you can accept that I might not be able to give you blow jobs as often as you like. But in the meantime, I think that we should experiment with some different positions and ways to put less stress on my jaw."

"I like the sound of that."

It definitely kept things interesting between the two of us. Leah tried giving me a blow job a few times but she would stop short of deep throating. That was fine with me because whatever she was doing, it turned me on, and we'd finish off some other way. She started to get creative with her hands and lots of lube. I was like her patient and willing "test subject" and it paid off. She somehow managed to use her mouth, lips, and hands in a way that felt very much like a blow job. She was amazing and she literally blew me away.

Holiday Make Up or Break Up

(TARA)

Sebastian and I had been dating for about two months when he went away to Brazil to handle some business he had over there. In the beginning, we talked regularly over the phone or via Skype video chat, but lately we barely even spoke once a week. It has been a month since he'd left and his absence was taking a toll on me. We were becoming so distant and living separate lives. My job had started to feel more burdensome and I tried to keep busy by doing productive things with my free time.

For Thanksgiving, since my parents had decided to go on a Caribbean cruise, I had decided to volunteer at a local homeless shelter instead of going away or to a friend's home for dinner. You'd think that it would be depressing to be around destitute people on Thanksgiving. Well, it was certainly eye opening, and at the risk of sounding cliché, it did actually made me feel thankful for what I have and to even have a job to complain about.

Volunteering at the homeless shelter, I learned that "they," the homeless, are not all that different from you or me. Many of these people are just regular folks, but they had fallen down on their luck. Some had lost their jobs or had gotten downsized. Then, when they ran through their savings and couldn't make their rent or mortgage payments, they lost their homes or ended up getting evicted. But when this happened, they had no safety net, no family support, and nowhere to go.

Once homeless, those who still had jobs ran into difficulties keeping them. Shelters were not always the safest or cleanest places to stay. Imagine being constantly on the move and without a clean shower or permanent address. These are just some of the challenges they faced. And what about those who didn't have jobs and were looking for employment?

Imagine how difficult it would be to get a job without proper hygiene or clothing, and no address or phone number? I met a single mother of two young children who had been living in a shelter with her kids. She was doing the best she could to just keep her kids with her through this difficult time. It made me think of my biological mother and what she must have had to go through to make the decision she had, leaving me at an orphanage in Thailand.

Thanksgiving marks the beginning of the countdown to Christmas and now that it was already December, things seemed to accelerate even more. But I still wasn't particularly in the Christmas mood. I had also started wondering, what was the point of being in this supposed relationship with Sebastian if most of our time was spent apart and not actually together.

The holidays were fast approaching and we hadn't yet made any plans to spend it together yet, so I just wanted the holidays to be over with and for the New Year to come. It was depressing to think of being alone around the holidays. That's when I decided to volunteer for the Nomi Network. I'd been receiving e-newsletters from them since hearing about them at Terence's film screening event. The Nomi Network's mission of eradicating sex trafficking resonated with me. I had a lot of questions about my mother and I didn't know if my mother was Cambodian or Thai. I've often wondered, what if I had never been adopted, what would my life be like now?

So, I offered to volunteer at the Nomi Network's holiday gift booth on Sunday afternoons. I would be helping to sell handmade purses and bags made by survivors and women at risk of sex trafficking. It was a part of their "Buy her bag not her body" products. One hundred percent of the profits earned from the sales of the purses and bags would be reinvested in career development, and training programs for women.

About a week into December, Sebastian called saying that he had a surprise for me, "Hi babe! How are you?"

"I'm good. What's new?" I replied.

"Well, I wanted to let you know that I'm going to be back in about a week and I'd really like for us to spend Christmas together."

Sweet Sebastian. I wondered how I'd doubted him. This was something to look forward to. "Oh that's great!"

"And that's not all, I have a surprise for you," he continued.

"What? What's the surprise?" I said excitedly.

"Well, I wanted to plan a trip for us to go to Mexico. What do you think of spending Christmas at a resort on the beach in Mexico? I think we both need to get away."

"Really? That sounds wonderful!" I was overjoyed. I imagined the sand under my feet and gorgeous turquoise blue waters.

"Can you arrange to take the week before Christmas off? Just clear your schedule and I'll take care of the rest."

Sebastian and I had never been away together on a trip for that long. We had done weekend trips together, so I was a little anxious but really looking forward to the opportunity for us to reconnect.

True to his word, the week before Christmas Sebastian and I flew to Cancun together. Upon our arrival at the airport in Cancun I immediately felt a sense of calm. As I looked around everyone seemed to be in vacation mode and I mean everyone, not just the tourists. I could see it in the way people were dressed and I could feel it in the pace of things. Our driver from the hotel resort was dressed in Bermuda shorts, flip flops, and a Hawaiian shirt. He drove us to the resort in Playa del Carmen.

The resort was very secluded with a private beach. Our room was one of the several private "huts" sprinkled among the palm trees behind the beach. The walls looked as though they were made of terra cotta clay. The ceramic tiles in the shower stall had colorful, hand-painted floral motifs, and the ceramic sink was also hand-painted with the same vibrant flowers. Outside of our door was a little wooden porch with two hammocks suspended from above. There were no televisions or Internet access in any of the rooms. It was just the right prescription for rest and relaxation.

"Remember, there is only one rule during our vacation," Sebastian said adamantly. "There is to be no talk about work and no complaining. We will just be in the moment and enjoy ourselves."

We filled the days lounging on the beach, in between snorkeling and scuba diving. One day Sebastian rented a car and we drove to see the Mayan ruins. We strolled around town like tourists, peeked into shops with silver jewelry created by local artisans and admired hand-painted porcelain items. I felt as if no time had passed between us.

Over dinner on the last night, Sebastian and I were snuggled at a private, little table at the resort's open-air restaurant. Under the moonlight by the fire of burning bamboo tiki torches, everything was aglow. It was all very cozy; that was the feeling of the entire trip— cozy.

"Okay, I am going to break my own rule. Tell me, how has work been? I know how unhappy you've been," Sebastian asked.

"Well, I realized that I've been unhappy at work even before I'd met you. The recession has really changed the nature of the business and the company culture. The one thing that has given me some sense of purpose is working with the Nomi Network. I love being a part of all the great work they are doing and helping them further their mission. The organization is run by a very dedicated team of people who have full-time jobs, in addition to working with the Nomi Network. Essentially, each of them has two full-time jobs."

"Tara, your face just lights up when you talk about the Nomi Network. You should stay involved or find some way to get more involved! I don't mean that you should give up your day job. Clearly, you can't do that, but maybe you can find another job where you'll be happier with better hours, and still do work with Nomi," Sebastian suggested.

"True, I guess if I got myself in a better place work-wise then I'd be able to do more for the Nomi Network," I responded.

"I can see why this is so important. In a way, it is bringing you back to your roots. You should also really consider going on the Nomi Network annual trip to Cambodia that you told me about. See what this organization is really about; meet Nomi and other survivors of sex trafficking; get to know all the board members and dedicated volunteers of the Nomi Network. And, you should go to Thailand while you're at it."

"At times I've felt like I just wanted to quit my job, but then what would be next? I realize that I don't need to make a career change because I still love my field of work, but I need to find the right place for myself where I'll be able to shine and enjoy my work again."

The vacation was just what we needed to reconnect. I felt like we were finally getting back on track. When we got back to New York, Sebastian was only able to stay for a day before he had to return to Brazil. On the day before his flight to Brazil, we met for dinner. Sebastian talked about his business and everything he'd been working on in Brazil.

I sensed that there was more, and then he dropped the bomb. He had decided to move there permanently. I was not sure where he was going with this and said, "What does this mean for us? Why did you wait until now to tell me? You don't expect me to visit or to consider moving there with you?"

"I don't feel comfortable asking you to do that. It's a huge responsibility for me to ask you to do that since I will be very busy with my business and I am the only person who you will know there. I don't want you to be miserable down there on account of me. Besides, your life is here."

"So, why did you go to all the trouble of planning the trip to Mexico for Christmas?"

"I didn't think it was the right time to break up right before the holidays," Sebastian said.

"But before New Year's Eve is the right time?"

"I'm sorry but I couldn't help that. I thought that the Mexico trip would be a great way for us to end things on a good note."

"These things never end on a good note," I shot back. I felt like it had all been a charade, "Well I wouldn't want you to pretend to be a couple on New Year's Eve," I added feeling disheartened.

What I'd hoped would have been an opportunity to make up turned out to be a break up. But we hadn't been in a real relationship for some time. The writing was on the wall now. The two of us were going in different directions. I couldn't just uproot myself and drop everything for him. I knew that I would miss him once he went off to Brazil again, but this time there would be no more waiting, wondering, or expectations. It was over. At least the distance between us would force us to move on and make it somewhat easier for things to just fade away.

The PJ Party

(TARA and Roxanne)

Two days after Sebastian left for Brazil, two of my friends, Celine and Sylvia, arrived on my doorstep. Celine was a petite brunette who had a feminine, elegant, understated style. Sylvia, on the other hand, dressed in very edgy, modern style. Both women used to live in New York and whenever they came to New York, they stayed with me. I gladly found myself busy and distracted in their flurry of activity—Sylvia wanted to check out some Indie rock band on the Lower East Side. And Celine wanted to go to a sample sale.

Celine lived in Shanghai and Sylvia in Geneva. Both were in New York to celebrate New Year's Eve. However, they had thought that I would be spending New Year's with Sebastian, so they had already made plans to go to a small intimate New Year's Eve party hosted by their friend, Gordon.

My New Year's Eve plans were completely up in the air now. I could have joined Celine and Sylvia, but instead I decided that I wanted to celebrate in a big way and to go all out. My plan was to go to a swanky New Year's Eve bash held at an exclusive loft space in the Flatiron District, organized by one of my event-planner friends. There would be plenty of gourmet appetizers, an open bar, a champagne toast, and a live band. I had immediately started inviting all of my single friends, who I knew would be notoriously last minute about making plans for New Year's Eve.

Roxanne was the first to enthusiastically reply, "I've missed the energy and nightlife of New York since moving to Boston a few months ago." Next was Melinda, another ex-New Yorker, who was now living in Austin. "Count me in," she said. Melinda had always had a plain, simple style. Usually she didn't wear any makeup.

However, when she went out for a night on the town, she would dramatically transform her look by wearing risqué outfits, fake eyelashes, colored contacts, and hair extensions.

On New Year's Eve day, Roxanne and Melinda arrived. The two of them, along with Celine and Sylvia would also be crashing at my place on New Year's Eve. Soon, my apartment was buzzing with activity as all five of us women started prepping and primping for New Year's Eve.

Being single on New Year's Eve might seem to some like the equivalent of being stag on prom night, but Roxanne, Melinda, and I danced the night away without a care about whom we'd be kissing at midnight. We were impervious to the advances of men that night because it was not enough to simply have someone to kiss at midnight, but it was about kissing the right person. Somewhere, deep down inside, each of us believed the old saying that the person you kiss at the stroke of midnight is the person you'll end up with in the New Year.

New Year's Eve is never really about the actual party, but the people you spend it with. With each passing year, it seemed more or less the same, with the same happy New Year tiaras, hats, and noisemakers, a countdown to the ball drop in Times Square, and a traditional champagne toast at midnight. One could almost imagine the simultaneous clinking of champagne glasses at the stroke of midnight all across the island of Manhattan. That night, as the clock struck midnight, the explosion of cascading fireworks would begin. And then it would continue like a domino effect across the globe as fireworks in each time zone were televised.

When the clock struck midnight, Roxanne, Melinda, and I hugged each other on the dance floor. Huddled in a big group hug, we kissed one another as we wished one another a happy New Year. Then, the happy New Year text messages started flying back and forth.

Celine and Sylvia sent me a photo from Gordon's party with the caption reading:

Here's to a fabulous New Year, Tara. May it be the best year yet! XO XO

About 3 A.M., Roxanne, Melinda, and I got back to my apartment. As we walked in, we saw Celine and Sylvia sprawled on the queen-sized air mattress that they were going to sleep on in the living room. They were chatting, already dressed in their PJs, makeup removed, looking like college students.

Roxanne, Melinda, and I were still a bit buzzed. We kicked off our shoes, plopped ourselves on the couches in the living room and listened to Sylvia who was talking about her on-again off-again relationship with a guy who lived in France. It had been a frustrating long distance relationship. Celine, on the other hand, loved the energy of Shanghai, but found it hard to date there.

"If you think it's hard to date in New York City, people in Shanghai are even more transient, and I've found some Shanghainese women super aggressive when it comes to dating and snagging a man," Celine complained.

"I hear ya, but it can't be worse than what I've been through lately with the whole online dating thing," Roxanne commiserated.

"Oh, do tell. Roxanne always has these stories," I giggled. "What's the latest story?"

"Recently, I'd started talking to this guy online through some dating website. We exchanged a few emails and then we started to IM. It was fun, flirtatious, and seemingly harmless. Then, he started joking around saying that when we finally met in person, he'd like to kiss me right away, just to get that over with and out of the way.

He said, 'I really, really want to kiss you. If I were there with you right now, I'd kiss you. I'd kiss you on the lips right this minute.' "

"Are you serious?" asked Celine.

Melinda, who was reclined on the couch that she was going to sleep on that night, said, "I think that's kind of cute." She tried to suppress a yawn.

"I told him, 'I don't know if I'd let you kiss me on the lips right away. I'll have to see.' " Roxanne paused, "And then he said, 'Well, if not those lips, maybe the *other* lips.' "

"Oh no, really?!" I exclaimed, my eyes widening.

"Yes, he actually said that!"

Celine and Sylvia doubled over with laughter. Melinda smiled as she rested her eyes.

"Are you serious?! What was he thinking? Did he think that you'd say yes to that instead?" said Celine. "Maybe that's because saying something like that to a guy would have worked. If a woman said something like that to a guy, that's basically like offering him a BJ."

Everyone started laughing.

"You always get these really forward men hitting on you," I said to Roxanne.

"I always get the nice, clingy boys," said Melinda with her eyes closed. "Remember Gabe?" she asked me.

"Oh, he was harmless," I said.

Melinda propped her head in her hands and continued, "Well, so I met this guy and he seemed kind of interesting and intellectual. We went out for brunch and the conversation started getting philosophical. We got into this discussion about which came first, the chicken or the egg, air or trees and so on. So, then, he pulls out his phone and says, let's settle this by checking what The Book of Genesis in The Bible says."

"He was joking, right?" said Sylvia.

"No, he was dead serious; he actually took out his phone!"

"What? Did he have a Bible app or something?" Sylvia asked, making a joke.

Melinda laughed, "I don't know, maybe he did. I don't know if he was Jewish, Christian, or what, but I don't think it's a good idea to bring up religion on the first date."

"It sounds like maybe he was one of those people who like to get into a debate about things. Maybe it wasn't about religion," I suggested.

"Whatever the case, at that point, I was trying to make excuses to end the date after we finished eating brunch. I even told him that I had to go pick up some feminine products before meeting up with one of my friends later."

"Oh, good one," Roxanne said.

"But no, he wasn't dissuaded. He didn't get the hint. He offered to take me to the nearest drug store and to drive me to wherever I needed to go next!" Melinda turned on to her back and snuggled under the throw that had been draped on the couch.

"You'd never think guys could be clingy, but some of them are. I had an ex like that. He seemed to turn everything into an argument," Celine said. "You know who I'm talking about..." Celine's voice trailed off as she looked at Sylvia and me. The three of us exchanged knowing looks. Celine continued, "So, this one time I went out for a girls' night out and left him at home. He didn't have any plans and was up waiting for me when I got home. He asked me who was there and how it was. That's all fine. Then, I mentioned that the girlfriend of one of his friends was also there. So he said, 'Oh, so she left her boyfriend at home too.' And I said, 'Yeah he was sick or something.' And then my ex said, 'WHAT? You think that it's okay that she left him at home to go out partying with her girlfriends, when he was sick and all?!' " Celine paused, "Man, he was really upset about that. We even got into a huge argument over it. You'd think that I was the one who had left him home alone and 'abandoned' him while he was sick!"

"You think that's bad? Try coming home to find your live-in boy-friend having another woman cook dinner for him, in *your* kitchen with *your* pots and pans and everything," said Sylvia.

"Oh, that's horrible! If that were me, I'd be hitting someone over the head with a frying pan," said Roxanne.

"Which one would you be hitting? Your boyfriend or the other woman?" I asked laughing.

"Probably whoever I'd be able to hit first!" Roxanne declared.

"So, what did you actually end up doing?" Celine asked.

"I screamed at both of them and told them to get out immediately. People should know when it's time to go," Sylvia responded.

"Well, on that note, I think we'd better be getting to bed," I whispered pointing at Melinda who had fallen asleep on the couch. "She has an early morning flight," I said.

"I'm the last one still up so I guess I get to share the bed with you," Roxanne remarked.

Then, Roxanne and I walked to my bedroom to get ready for bed.

The Lucky Ring

(MONTOYA and Luana)

From the time I was a student at Oxford, I have had this sterling silver horseshoe ring that I wore on the middle finger of my right hand. I saw it in a shop in downtown London and I decided that it would be my good luck piece. I wore it all the time. I'd wear it with the horseshoe facing up, never down. I had read that this would keep luck coming in all the time.

Essentially, this ring had been permanently attached to my hand for nearly twenty years. Then, one day, while I was at Luana's for a private birthday gathering, sipping a drink, I was shocked to look down and see that the ring had disappeared off my hand. I felt more and more agitated as I looked all over for it, retracing all my steps around Luana's apartment over and over again. I hadn't been drinking a lot, but I could not find the ring. It was as if it had disappeared into another dimension of the universe.

Luana had noticed me searching around for something, and asked me if I had dropped something, so I told her, "I'm looking around for my lucky ring."

"Your lucky horseshoe ring? I can't believe you've lost it," she said.

"Blimey! I can't believe it either. I keep that ring on all the time. I sleep with it on and I've never taken it off except to shower, for nearly twenty years! Bloody bad luck if you ask me."

"Don't worry about it. I will search tomorrow after everyone has left. However, if I can't find it, I have a ring for you," Luana said as if she had a secret.

"What does that mean?"

"It's just what I said. Don't get another ring. I have a ring for you. Have lunch with me tomorrow and I will give you a new ring."

"Okay," I said somewhat apprehensively.

The next day I met her at Cafeteria in Chelsea. After sitting down, Luana handed me a ring, but not in the usual manner. It wasn't in a box. She just handed it to me as if it had been removed from someone's hand. It was solid 18 karat gold with a beautiful blue sapphire surrounded by four diamonds. The ring was obviously very expensive, costing several thousands of dollars. My lucky ring on the other hand was inexpensive and was probably worth less than 100 dollars.

"I don't understand. Did you just have this ring lying around your flat?" I asked.

"I have had it for seven years. I had given it to my brother. But he plays the piano and he didn't like wearing it. So, when I saw he wasn't wearing it, I asked for it back. Since then, it's been in my closet for seven years. So, now, it's yours. I know that you wore the ring that you lost for good luck but this one is much better. Do you know anything about gemstones?"

"No, not really," I replied.

"I've read about the subject. Sapphires have always been associated with divine favor in every great civilization of the past. So, wearing this will be luckier than the horseshoe ring. With the horseshoe, you just get luck, but with this ring, you will get God's blessings."

"I didn't know you were religious."

"Well, I don't practice any organized religion, but I do believe there is probably some sort of a God or Spirit or Creator—call it what you will."

I thanked her for the gift and had the ring resized for my middle right finger. I kept it on all the time just like I did with the horseshoe ring. A week later, Luana and I met for a drink at the King Cole bar.

"This is for you," I said handing her a small gift box.

She opened it with curiosity and inside was a beautiful opal pendant with a gold chain.

"This belonged to my sister. I don't tell this to a lot of people, but she passed away twenty years ago. I thought that since you gave me the sapphire ring, that I should give you something nice also."

"I am so sorry for your loss Montoya and I really thank you for such a beautiful and sentimental gift. This is really beautiful." Then, Luana added, "I just realized, I gave you something that belonged to my brother. Now, you have given me something that belonged to your sister. This makes us family. We are family now."

"See, my luck has improved already," I said as I hugged my new-found sister.

Tequila Surprise

(NINE)

Since Ragnar and I had broken up, I had been in a downward spiral, and things spun out of control when I learned about my cousin Trent's sex videos. It caused me to question God and wonder why I should bother being a good girl. I had also started to feel hornier than ever. Lately, it seemed like every date I had with a guy, I ended up French kissing him. I even let some guys touch my boobies. Then, I started bringing guys home and giving them blow jobs, even though I had vowed to stop doing that after Randy.

All the while, I was thinking of Ragnar, and to how we had been such good Christians and on our best behavior, but it hadn't worked out. I started to think that maybe I should just give up my virginity. It had always been such a burden and now I would get rid of it once and for all. The perfect candidate would be someone who was experienced but discrete. I knew what I was looking for.

I never really dated Asians before, and then I met Rong Ren at my friend Harrison's birthday party at the Empire Hotel bar. He was a violinist in a philharmonic orchestra and he was definitely attractive and had an air of confidence and sophistication. He seemed like a gentleman and was totally at ease with me. Since he had toured all over the world with the philharmonic, he had dated women of many different nationalities. It turns out that he was quite the ladies' man. So, when I told him that I was half-black and half-German, he said that he had never dated that particular combination. He also made a joke that now that he had met a "Nine," he wanted to meet all the other numbers also.

"I've dated practically every type of woman in North America, with only one exception. Everyone but an Eskimo," he said.

"Why not an Eskimo?" I asked.

"Because they are mainly in the Arctic Circle and I haven't been there yet."

"Here's a tip for you. I think the better term would be *Inuit*, not Eskimo. That's something to keep in mind if you have any hope of scoring with one," I informed him in good humor.

Since it was Harrison's birthday, I ordered a round of tequila shots and encouraged Rong to do a shot with me. He told me he didn't handle liquor well and made me promise to look after his violin. He had his violin with him since he had come straight from practicing at the Lincoln Center nearby.

"Make sure you look after my violin. It is very expensive and has been in my family for generations," he said looking at me intensely.

"Definitely, I promise."

"You have to swear to God," he insisted.

"Okay, I swear to God I will make sure that I look after your violin."

So, we had one tequila shot, then two. Somewhere along the line, I stopped counting. We were both sloshed when I suggested we go back to my place. This was it. I was going to actually have sex for the first time. This was the guy. He seemed harmless enough and I could look back at this and be glad I had done it. We started to leave the bar and I remembered to tell him "Hey, don't forget your violin." He took it and we hailed a cab.

We French kissed and he laid me down on the cab seat, unbuttoned my blouse, and removed my bra and started kissing my boobies and licking my nipples. The cab driver yelled at us three times before we stopped our making out and realized we were at my address. I hastily put my bra back on and buttoned up my blouse. As we waited for the elevator, I rifled through my purse to find my keys. Then, when we were in the elevator he put his hand up my skirt feeling up my ass.

In my apartment, we both immediately took off our clothes and lay on my bed. I kept thinking... this is it! This is it! A part of me felt like I was finally having my independence from Ragnar, God, and everyone else who wanted me to be a good girl. He got off the bed to pull out a condom from his pants when a look came over his face that to this day still haunts me. It was a look of sheer panic and dread as if his entire life had suddenly vanished in one quick moment.

"Where is my violin?" he asked in a low voice as if he were asking the universe and not me.

Two naked people in an apartment, one with a condom still in his hand, the other realizing that this was a moment she would never forget the rest of her life.

"Where is my violin?!" he repeated, this time yelling.

"I think we left it in the cab," I said reluctantly, suddenly realizing what had happened.

"Where is my violin?! Where is my violin?! You promised to look after it! You promised!" He kept repeating himself as he started to frantically run around the apartment. Soon, he was opening closet doors and looking underneath my furniture and behind my bookshelves.

"Calm down, Rong, Let's try to figure out what to do," I said to him, but I really had no idea what to do. Of course, I hadn't noticed the cab's medallion number and I certainly didn't have a receipt from the cab. I vaguely remembered Rong hastily handing the cabbie some cash.

"I know it's got to be around here somewhere!" he screamed as he started rummaging through my things, flipping things around, and then he started throwing things left and right.

I was afraid so I ran into the bathroom with my cell phone and called 911. I also knew that I had a bathrobe hanging in there that I could put on to cover myself up. I heard the sound of glass crashing as I continued to hide in the bathroom. The police, I am happy to say, arrived ten minutes later to find a naked violinist in my apartment, which now looked like a tornado had hit it.

At first the police were confused about what had happened because Rong was ranting about how he couldn't find his violin and that it was all my fault. I explained to the police that Rong had rummaged through my apartment looking for the violin, but that it had actually been accidentally left in a taxi earlier that night and now I wanted Rong to leave. The police told Rong that either he would have to leave with them or he would be arrested. He hadn't assaulted me but had ransacked my apartment. Finally, the police convinced Rong to get dressed and as he left my apartment, he gave me a look like he wanted to kill me.

He was right. I had violated his trust. I had promised and sworn to God to look after his violin and, instead, had left it in the cab after deliberately getting him drunk. All of this had happened just so that I could have sex for the first time.

Exhausted from the whole ordeal, I went to my bathroom, which was practically the only area in my apartment that was not a complete mess. I sat on the toilet crying uncontrollably. Finally, I left the bathroom and cleared a place on the floor in the mess that used to be my bedroom. I got down on my knees and said, "Dear God. I am a sinner and I know that this situation had your hand in it. I am so, so sorry for being weak and wanting to just get rid of my virginity so hastily. I am so sorry for hurting this innocent man, Rong. I am truly sorry for being so self-centered. I will repent as best as I can."

I didn't want anyone to know what had happened, but my neighbors had come out when they heard all the banging from Rong throwing around things and moving my furniture. But at least, Montoya didn't know and neither did anyone at The Journey. I will lay low and try to figure out how to deal with all this.

Postscript: A couple of days later, I sat and wrote Rong Ren a very long apology note; it was stained with the tears that I had streaming down my face as I wrote it. I sent it to him with a first-class round trip plane ticket to Alaska.

A Perfect Nine

(NINE and Montoya)

The intercom in my apartment buzzed, but I wasn't expecting anyone, and I hadn't ordered any food. Reluctantly, I answered it. My doorman had told me that it was Montoya. He had left me a few voicemails, but I hadn't returned any of them. So, I decided to let him come up.

As he entered my apartment, he had a look of surprise and shock, though he had been in my apartment many times. Normally, I kept it neat and organized, but now there were old pizza boxes and Chinese take-out boxes lying around. I had been crying nonstop and didn't have any energy to clean up the offending evidence. I guess I didn't realize how bad the place looked until I saw the expression on Montoya's face.

"I wanted to drop by to check up on you. I knew something was wrong when you didn't show up for work; then, I got worried—especially when you didn't respond to my voicemails. But I didn't expect this. This place is a disaster and sorry to say this, but you look a mess."

"I haven't left the apartment in a few days," I responded.

"A few days? Seriously, it looks like a few weeks. Is this just about Ragnar or is it because it's Valentine's Day tomorrow, or is it something more?"

"Yes, it's about my whole life," I paused and reached for a tissue to blow my nose and sat on the couch. I looked at Montoya and paused not knowing how he'd react to what I was about to say. "Do you know that I am a virgin?" I confessed.

"Wow! That is some conversation starter. Let me sit down for this one," Montoya said. "I didn't expect to hear you tell me this since I have seen you getting quite friendly with guys at parties."

"I definitely haven't been entirely pure. I have done things I am not proud of. But I have never done intercourse."

"Really? So you are a real virgin?"

"Can you be a fake virgin?"

"I guess not. So, why are you telling me this?"

"Lately, I've been wondering, should I just do it? I know that you really care about me and only want the best for me. I trust your advice. I am trying to be a good Christian but I keep asking myself why am I waiting for marriage?"

"Now, Nine, as you know I was raised Christian but I stopped going to church a long time ago. I am definitely not a virgin. So, why not ask one of your Christian friends at The Journey Church?"

"I want your advice. You give good advice. Is it wrong to be a virgin?"

"No. Absolutely not. I think it is very admirable and it shows how spiritual and devoted you are."

"So, why do people act like I am some kind of freak or leper? Remember my friend Belinda? She kept introducing me to friends as her 'innocent little sister.' "

"I remember you telling me this, but I didn't realize that meant a virgin. Well, I am glad you got rid of her as a friend. That isn't right—her poking fun at you. Look, if you are happy being a virgin that is all that counts. Find yourself a nice Christian guy and get married. Doesn't your church have hundreds of single Christian guys?"

"Yeah, but I haven't found Mr. Right yet. Tell me, you're not a virgin. Should I wait?"

"I think that your personality," Montoya paused thinking of the right words to say, "With your personality, yes, you should wait. I think you would be very disappointed in yourself if you gave in to lust. You've waited this long. You can wait another year or two," Montoya said as he leaned over and gave me a hug. It felt good being held by a guy again. I felt safe around Montoya.

"Aren't you my Nine?"

"I wonder when I'm going to meet a guy who genuinely cares about me like you do," I said as I started to cry again to the point of gasping and sobbing, feeling more and more sorry for myself.

"What is really wrong?" Montoya asked, this time realizing how vulnerable I truly was.

"It seems like God doesn't want me to date. Maybe, he does. I really don't know. All I know is that all of this has me thinking that maybe I should give up on dating totally!"

"Don't you think that is overreacting just a tad?"

Then, I looked at him as I felt tears streaming down my eyes and told him about the police incident with the lost violin, and how it was so humiliating. I also told him about Trent and his secret sex tapes. Afterward, I immediately felt relieved.

"I had no idea that you've been going through all this. You know that you can always talk to me about things. I wish that you had come to me with all this," Montoya said reassuring me as he gave me a big hug.

"I feel like these are all signs that God doesn't want me to lose my virginity. I should wait!" I cried as Montoya reached to hug me again. "Yes, I should wait!"

"Until that time, date a lot, and be very picky about who you go for. Remember, you are a 'Perfect Nine' and you are worth waiting for."

"Calling 911 was the last straw! I'm not sure what God wants, but it has all been too much for me! Of course, I still want to date but I feel like God is some big mystery up in the sky. I keep trying to figure out what he wants. It feels like a choice—like I have to make a choice between God or dating."

Montoya was silent for a while. "I really am at a loss for words," he said.

"I need your help. I feel like I need to do something very drastic. Would you do something for me, as a close friend of yours?"

"Of course, I would. I would do anything for you, my little Nine," Montoya responded.

"Now, don't think that I am crazy, but I have an idea. I've heard about the Jerusalem Syndrome. It happens to people when they go to Jerusalem. It has a powerful effect on most people. Many people have religious experiences and many people who are having a crisis of faith find God again there. Some people end up crying a lot when they are there and feel God's presence."

"What does that have to do with your 911 call?"

"It might seem like a radical idea, but let's go there this weekend. Let's leave this weekend and take Monday and Tuesday off from work. Please come with me to the Holy Land. My treat!"

"Are you out of your bloody mind?! Going to Israel? It's dangerous there. Maybe some suicide bomber will blow you up and that would be the end of your virgin problem," Montoya said without thinking. "I have to admit, I never thought of that as a solution."

"I am serious. I am going to go to Israel this weekend."

"You're serious?"

"I am very serious."

"Nine, listen to me," Montoya said putting his hand on my shoulder and looking at me intently. "I saw an episode of *The Simpsons* TV show spoofing the Jerusalem Syndrome. It made me curious, so, I looked into it. Everyone responds differently to the Jerusalem Syndrome. You're right that many people have emotional experiences and feel closer to God. But what is truly frightening is that some people hear voices and a very small percentage of people even go off their rocker."

"I don't know what will happen. All I know is that I have a gut feeling that God wants me to go there," I said with certainty.

"But you could become one of those people who goes bonkers and begin to think that you are a Biblical character or even crazier stuff than that," Montoya warned. "You could become a barking lunatic."

"Montoya, I am willing to take that chance. I am going and I really need you to come with me. Please come with me. I can't do this alone," I pleaded. "You've always supported me and have been my mentor, a brother, really. You're my only family in New York. I can't do this without you. I am at my wit's end."

Montoya looked at me as he considered what I had just said. "Let's make a pact between the two of us. If you go bonkers, I will take care of you and you will do the same for me. But just in case we both go bonkers, we should tell someone about our plans."

"Well, I don't want anyone to really know about this. But if it makes you feel more comfortable about going, I will tell my cousin, Hosea. He knows how my faith was challenged by what I learned about Trent after his passing, but I obviously won't go into the other details. Would that be okay with you?"

"Yes, that works."

"But you really shouldn't worry. I've read that many people don't feel anything at all when they visit Jerusalem. However, I am just hoping I am one of those who will go there and feel closer to God."

Montoya paused looking into my eyes. "Nine, I love you. Of course, I will go with you, but we should each pay for ourselves then." Montoya paused again and said, "I love you and I'll be there for you."

"Thanks! This means so much to me and I love you too!"

The Jerusalem Syndrome

(MONTOYA and Nine)

Nine and I got on the Saturday evening El Al flight to Tel Aviv from JFK airport. The flight was more than ten hours long and we both slept on the plane. Nine had booked a room at a luxurious hotel in Herzliya, a posh suburb of Tel Aviv. It was only twenty-five minutes away from the airport by car.

Although Nine agreed that we each pay for our own flights, she insisted on paying for my room. So, I suggested that she not spend so much and that she and I share a room with two double beds. I also insisted that she dress in pajamas to make sure that we weren't tempted, well that I wasn't tempted to go beyond the bounds of our platonic relationship. "No Victoria's Secret's lingerie," I said making a joke.

Nine was a little peeved that we didn't have enough time to visit the Pyramids in nearby Egypt. As a little girl, she had always wanted to see them. It was a childhood dream of hers and despite the danger caused by recent events, it made her feel upset to know that she'd be so close and yet so far. However, the main purpose of our trip was to visit Jerusalem and we only had a couple of days.

When we arrived, it was Sunday afternoon. As I had never been to Israel before, I was unprepared for the difference between my anticipated fears versus the actual reality. I thought that in Israel, everyone would be stressed out from the constant conflict, but Tel Aviv definitely had a peaceful feeling to it. All the cabs were white and so were most of the cars there. I guess they were white to reflect the sun. What a big contrast to all the yellow cabs in New York.

We started our afternoon at the Herzliya beach and then took a cab to the beach in Tel Aviv, where we noticed that most people were doing some sort of physical activity like playing volleyball, running, or swimming. Every half a mile of beach there was an open air exercise space with all sorts of workout equipment for people to use. People were out running with their dogs like a scene out of that TV show *Baywatch*. Nine and I couldn't believe all the eye candy.

"People have told me that Tel Aviv reminded them of Miami Beach. I definitely have to agree. I can't believe how beautiful the women in Tel Aviv are," I said in disbelief.

"I know. It's not just the women. I was never that attracted to Jewish guys before, but maybe that's because I never saw these ones. But then again, maybe if the Jewish guys in New York were as tanned and fit, I'd go for them. Women are always asking me where they can meet hot guys. Now, I can tell them that I know where all the hot guys are," Nine paused. "In Tel Aviv."

"Seriously, I could sit for hours taking in all the gorgeous women in little bikinis on this beach. From all the news I've seen on the BBC, I was expecting tanks in the streets, not stunning women in bikinis. I didn't expect this at all."

On the morning of the second day, we arranged for a car service to take us from our hotel to Jerusalem, which was one hour away. There we would be joining a tour group. Our tour guide, an old Jewish guy in his seventies, knew more about Jesus than both Nine and I put together. History seemed to come alive in Jerusalem. Everything from The Bible now had a visual image attached to it.

I saw young Israeli women soldiers who looked like high school students. They didn't seem any older than eighteen or nineteen years old. Nine took a photo for me as I posed with three young women in soldier uniforms. I always pictured soldiers in their thirties or forties, like John Wayne in *The Sands of Iwo Jima*, but all the soldiers in Israel were young, very young.

Our first day in Jerusalem didn't allow us to see the old city so we made a short trip to visit the Yad Vashem Holocaust Museum. I had visited the Holocaust Museum in Washington, D.C. before, but in comparison Yad Vashem seemed massive. Seeing one gruesome image after another will bring a tear to anyone's eyes. Nine had tears in her eyes for the entire four hours we were in the museum. It seems unbelievable that humans could be so cruel to each other. The World War II section made me think of the Blitz back home and how two of my relatives had died as a result.

When we got back to Herzliya, we had enough time to enjoy the Tel Aviv nightlife, so we did some bar hopping and wound up at a dance club. The nightlife scene reminded me a little of Miami Beach and New York City. While we were at the club, I went to the men's room and returned to find Nine being talked up by three hot Tel Aviv men. She gave me a look that told me that she was fine. She seemed to be happy and enjoying the attention so I hung back at the bar.

As I was enjoying my gin and tonic, a gorgeous woman came over to talk to me. I talked to her while keeping a watchful eye on Nine. At the end of the evening, Nine had the contact information for the three men and I had the woman's. I like this city!

The next morning we were jarred awake by a wake-up call from the car service. The driver was waiting for us and wondering where we were. Obviously, we'd had a little too much fun the night before, but we were still able to quickly get ready and make it to Jerusalem in time to meet up with our tour group. First, we visited the Garden of Gethsemane, where Judas betrayed Jesus. Next was the Church of the Holy Sepulchre, which was packed with tourists. Historically, it is the place Christians believe Jesus was crucified, buried, and resurrected. Because of this, many priests, nuns, and church groups visit this holy site.

The entire city of old Jerusalem was divided into four parts, the Muslim Quarter, the Christian Quarter, the Jewish Quarter, and the Armenian Quarter. Each quarter was filled with vendors selling their wares. As Nine and I walked through each of the quarters, we bought a few souvenirs for our friends and family. I had seen so many tears shed over the last two days at Yad Vashem, the Garden of Gethsemane, and the Church of the Holy Sepulchre. You'd think that this might make you feel somber, but that was yet to come.

I was totally unprepared for our next stop, which was at the Wailing Wall. The Wall is the last remaining wall of the Jew's former temple. Now, the Muslim Dome of the Rock sits on top of where the temple used to be. The mosque was off-limits to non-Muslims so Nine and I couldn't visit it. The Wailing Wall was divided into a men's and women's section. Men were on the left and women were on the right. Women had to wear a head covering like a scarf or a shawl and men had to wear a skullcap or what Jews call a yarmulke.

Nine and I separated as she went to the women's section and I went to the men's section. Many men were at the Wall, rocking back and forth as they prayed. I watched as some of the men inserted slips of paper on which prayer requests were written into the cracks of the wall. Though I had seen the image of the Wailing Wall on television before, I had no idea that there is an inner enclosed section on the men's side. I went into this section. Most of the men there were orthodox looking, with the long curls on the side of their heads and they wore long coats. Some of them wore furry hats as head coverings while others wore yarmulkes.

I closed my eyes, put both of my hands on the wall and just stood there motionless for a while. I hadn't prayed for years and just tried to absorb what I was feeling. Then, I heard a small distinct whisper in both of my ears. I opened my eyes and looked around to see who was there, but no one was standing near me. I closed my eyes again and the whispering resumed. I wondered if I was imagining this. But I heard it over and over again, like a broken record. It was like those old records on an old-style phonograph player, when you had to put a coin on the needle to prevent it from repeating itself. It wasn't a male voice; it was a woman's voice, no actually a girl's voice. And the girl's voice kept repeating the same message: "Come back to him. He loves you."

Immediately, I thought who is "him" and why does he love me? But then, I realized who the voice belonged to and tears started welling up in my eyes. I couldn't understand why I was hearing her voice. Finally, I understood who "him" was and I broke down, crying very loudly. Some of the orthodox-looking men in the section came to me and put their hands on my shoulders trying to comfort me, not even knowing why I was crying so loudly. After a few minutes, I collected myself, and left to find Nine.

She looked startled when she saw me since it was obvious from my eyes that I had been crying. She hugged me and asked me what was wrong. I told her I couldn't talk about it and she let it go. In the car ride back to the hotel in Herzliya, Nine realized that I needed some space and so we sat in silence for the entire trip. Later, that night at dinner, we had some wine and feeling more relaxed, I finally decided to open up to Nine.

"I guess you are wondering why I was crying earlier?" I said.

"Listen Montoya, I don't want to pry. It's your business."

"As you know, I was raised a Christian. Both my parents were and still are devout Christians. Every Sunday we all went to All Soul's Church in central London, where John Stott used to preach. But I never told you why I stopped going to church. As a matter of fact, I've never told any of my New York friends why I stopped going to church and reading The Bible," I confessed.

"Well, you can always open up to me. I am here for you."

"This is difficult to talk about. I had a younger sister named Evie who died when I was seventeen years old."

"That's terrible. I'm sorry. I thought you were an only child. How old was she when she passed away?"

"She was fourteen years old. She was an angel. What a great soul. So loving and caring. She looked up to me and called me her 'big Archie bear.' " Tears started welling up in my eyes and Nine moved close to me and put her arms around me.

"She was run over by a drunk driver and she died instantly. There was a short trial and the driver went to jail for it. But it still didn't feel like justice to me. All the elders in the church told me 'It was God's will' and 'God wanted to call her home.' But to me, that was a complete load of rubbish! To me, there seemed no reason for it at all. Why kill so innocent a soul? My parents were heartbroken and at the funeral, they were sobbing uncontrollably, but I responded differently. I didn't even shed a tear. While my parents kept their faith, I just shut down. I felt that God had betrayed my trust. Why trust a God who can kill such an innocent life? I never read The Bible again or went to church again or prayed again. That was twenty years ago."

"I had no idea that this happened to you and your family. I'm so sorry for your loss Montoya," Nine said. Now, she was the one with tears in her eyes.

"Whatever grief I held in that day seems to be coming out today. At the Wailing Wall today, I heard Evie's voice whispering in my ears clear as day. She said 'Come back to him. He loves you.' " Nine reached over and put her hand on mine, as I continued, "Evie's voice kept repeating this message over and over again until I realized who 'him' was and then the whispering stopped. I finally realized that the 'him' is God."

"God?" Nine questioned with a look of surprise.

"I can't believe I came here to help you snap out of depression and I'm the one who gets the religious experience! Astounding!"

"I don't know what to say," Nine said in a whisper as she wiped away her tears.

"I have turned my back on God for two decades. But I will try to make a go of it again," I said with conviction.

"So, will you come with me to The Journey when we get back to New York? I've invited you many times and you always said, 'No thanks.' "

"Yes, I will definitely go."

"I can't believe how this turned out," Nine again had tears in her eyes. "Everything that I've been through has been for you, not me."

"Why do you say that?" I asked.

"My crisis of faith got you here and I didn't even know you had an even bigger crisis of faith than I was having. So, everything I'd been through, my breakup with Ragnar, my cousin's sex videos, the 911 call to get Rong out of my apartment, which led to my crisis of faith—it was all brought together by God to help you, my dear friend, to get your faith back," Nine said bringing clarity to the entire situation.

"Yes, I see that now," I said as I nodded in agreement and took in everything Nine had said. "I never would have traveled to Jerusalem if it wasn't to help you out."

"Somehow, all of my dating problems pale in comparison when I think of all that you've been through," Nine said.

"If I can give God another chance, so should you," I said feeling as if a burden had now been lifted.

The next day, on the flight back to New York, Nine seemed like she was getting back to her usual self—happy and positive. It seemed like my religious experience had given her hope for herself.

On the plane she declared, "I will come back to the Holy Land, and next time I will finally visit the Pyramids in Giza and the Burning Bush at Mount Sinai."

"Really? You mean THE Burning Bush? The one where Moses talked to God face-to-face like in the movie *The Ten Commandments*?"

"Yes, Ragnar told me about it. Just as they built a church over the spot where Jesus was resurrected, they also built a church over where they believe the actual Burning Bush is. It is called St. Catherine's Monastery, and it is right at the foot of Mount Sinai. You can actually see it in person."

"That's a great idea," I said to Nine, who looked the happiest I've seen her in a while.

TO BE CONTINUED in Metropolicks Book 3

ABOUT THE AUTHORS

Felicia Lin is a Taiwanese American writer who was born in Fairbanks, Alaska and raised in Ottawa, Ontario, Canada. She has a bachelor of science degree in Accounting from the University of Illinois at Champaign-Urbana and a master of arts degree in Applied Psychology from New York University. Currently, she resides in New York City. To learn more about her visit: www.felicialin.com.

Victor Scott Rodriguez is a native New Yorker, born in Brooklyn, and raised in Brooklyn, Queens and Manhattan. He has a bachelor's degree in Communications from Hunter College, a bachelor's degree in Religion from Rutgers University and a master of arts degree in Divinity from the University of Chicago Divinity School. Currently, he resides in New York City. To learn more about him visit: www.victorscottrodriguez.com.

Find Out What's Next for Metropolicks

VISIT www.Metropolicks.com

JOIN our mailing list to learn about events, news, and special offers.

WATCH us on 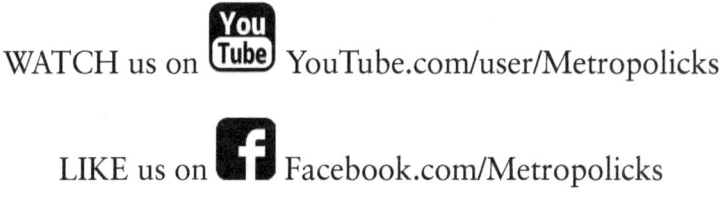 YouTube.com/user/Metropolicks

LIKE us on Facebook.com/Metropolicks

FOLLOW us on @Metropolicks

CONNECT with us on Linkedin.com/company/ Metropolicks

PIN us on Pinterest.com/Metropolicks

FOLLOW us on @Metropolicks

DISCLAIMER OF ENDORSEMENT

Reference contained in this novel to any specific commercial products(s), service(s) by trade name, trademark(s), manufacturer(s), organization(s), institutions(s), corporation(s), the appearance of external hyperlink(s), church(es), place(s) of worship or otherwise, does not necessarily constitute or imply its endorsement, recommendation, or favoring by any of the heretofore referenced or any governmental agencies. The views and opinions of the authors expressed herein do not necessarily state or reflect those of those commercial product(s), services(s) by trade name, trademark(s), manufacturer(s), organization(s), institution(s), corporation(s), the appearance of external hyperlink(s), church(es), place(s) of worship, governmental agencies or otherwise, and shall not be used for advertising or product endorsement purposes.

Neither of the authors has financial interest by the reference to any specific commercial product(s), services(s) by trade name, trademark(s), manufacturer(s), organization(s), institution(s), corporation(s), the appearance of external hyperlink(s), church(es), place(s) of workshop or otherwise nor has any specific commercial product(s), service(s) by trade name, trademark(s), manufacturer(s), organization(s), institution(s), corporation(s), the appearance of external hyperlinks(s), church(es), place(s) of worship or otherwise, paid any monies to the authors to be referred in the novel.

www.ingramcontent.com/pod-product-compliance
Lightning Source LLC
Chambersburg PA
CBHW050942120626
46552CB00001B/344